Macbeth

Annotation-Friendly Edition

William Shakespeare

firestonebooks.com

Macbeth
Annotation-Friendly Edition
William Shakespeare

2021 Edition

Published by Firestone Books

ISBN-13: 9781909608382

firestonebooks.com

You can also find out more by following Firestone Books on Facebook and Twitter

Contents

A Quick Guide to Successful Annotating

- Write down any thoughts you have as you go along
- Highlight key points, either with a highlighter or by underlining
- Note any literary techniques in the margins. (The *Glossary of Literary Terms* at the back of the book should help)
- Define any words you don't understand – it will help you later
- Look for patterns, such as repeating words and phrases
- Pick out key points that show a character's development
- Summarise your thoughts on the blank pages at the end of each act
- Once you've finished reading the play, go back and add to your notes. In particular look at foreshadowing, echoing and motifs

William Shakespeare

A Brief Biography

William Shakespeare was born in Stratford-upon-Avon, the son of John Shakespeare, a successful glove-maker, and Mary Arden, the daughter of a prosperous farmer. His date of birth is unknown but he was baptised, most likely within a few days of his birth, on 26th April 1564.

It is likely that Shakespeare attended the King's New School in Stratford-upon-Avon where he would have received a classical education. He did not attend university, and at the age of eighteen he married Anne Hathaway who was eight years his senior. Six months later, in May 1583, Anne gave birth to a daughter, Susanna. In 1585 Anne also gave birth to twins, Hamnet and Judith.

Between 1585 and 1592 almost nothing is known of Shakespeare's life, the so called "lost years". Many apocryphal tales about this period have been reported including that he fled his hometown for London to escape prosecution for deer poaching, that he started his theatrical career minding the horses of wealthy theatregoers, and that he may have been briefly employed as a schoolmaster in Lancashire.

By 1592 Shakespeare was an established playwright, with several of his plays having been staged in London. It is also the year that fellow playwright, Robert Greene, published his infamous *Groats-Worth of Wit* in which he attacked Shakespeare for trying to match the writing of university educated writers such as Christopher Marlowe and Thomas Nashe.

In 1596, Shakespeare's only son, Hamnet, died, and while in later years Shakespeare's daughters would marry and have four children between them, none of Shakespeare's grandchildren would have children of their own, and so in 1670 with the death of his granddaughter, Elizabeth, his

direct line was ended.

Shakespeare's plays were only performed by the Lord Chamberlain's Men, a company of actors, in which Shakespeare had a share. In 1599 some members of the Lord Chamberlain's Men built their own theatre on the south bank of the river Thames and named it the Globe. As a shareholder in this theatre, holding up to 3000 spectators, Shakespeare became a wealthy man.

Prior to 1599 Shakespeare had only written two tragedies: *Titus Andronicus* and *Romeo and Juliet*, with his focus being more on comedies, history plays and poems. After 1599 he almost stopped writing history plays and instead switched to writing tragedies, writing many of his finest plays including: *Hamlet, Othello, King Lear* and *Macbeth.*

In 1603 the new king, James I, awarded the Lord Chamberlain's Men a royal patent and the company changed its name to the King's Men.

As well as writing plays, Shakespeare also wrote two long poems and a collection of sonnets. The sonnets describe two love affairs, but who these lovers were – or even if they were real or imagined – remains a mystery.

As Shakespeare was also an actor, it meant that rather than working on his plays in isolation he would have worked closely with other actors. Many of the plots for the plays came from history books, or earlier Italian tales, so it is difficult, if not impossible, to work out what contributions were Shakespeare's. Even when he'd finished a particular play, it was still likely to be re-worked by actors and others – something that is done to this day, and keeps his work as fresh and interesting as its ever been.

Though Shakespeare worked as a writer and actor in London for most of his adult life, his did spend much of his time in Stratford-upon-Avon where, in 1597, he bought New Place as his family home. It's known that Shakespeare was still working as an actor in London in 1608, and that he also retired to Stratford 'some years before his death'.

Shakespeare died on the 23rd of April 1616, around the time of his 52nd birthday. It was said by John Ward, the vicar of Stratford, writing in the mid-1600s that 'Shakespeare, Drayton and Ben Johnson had a merry meeting and, it seems, drank too hard, for Shakespeare died of a fever there contracted.'

Shakespeare was buried at the Holy Trinity Church, the place of his baptism over half a century earlier. The epitaph on his gravestone has a curse against disturbing his resting place:

Good friend, for Jesus' sake forbear,
To dig the dust enclosed here.
Blessed be the man that spares these stones,
And cursed be he that moves my bones.

Fellow dramatist, Ben Johnson, famously and presciently referred to Shakespeare as being 'not of an age, but for all time.' Since his death Shakespeare's reputation has grown, leading him to now be widely regarded as the greatest writer in the English language and the world's greatest dramatist.

Introduction

Macbeth may be Shakespeare's shortest tragedy, but what it lacks in length it more than makes up for in power. Its theme is one of destruction brought about by ambition unchecked by moral constraints, and is something that is as resonant now as it was when first performed over four hundred years ago.

Many scholars believe the play to have been written around 1606, due to the play perhaps alluding to the gunpowder plot of 1605. Others have put the writing of the play as being as early as 1599. Of course, this play may have been written earlier and revised and re-revised by Shakespeare as time passed, thus causing confusion for scholars later on.

Spoiler alert – if you do not know what happens in *Macbeth* you may wish to stop reading the introduction now and return to it after reading the play.

There were a number of sources that Shakespeare is likely to have drawn on, when writing *Macbeth. Daemonologie* by King James, published in 1597 detailed the North Berwick Witch Trials of 1590, where the women on trial were recorded as having conducted rituals in the same manner as the three witches in *Macbeth.* In *Holinshead's Chronicles* a man named Donwald discovers that several of his family have been executed by King Duff. Donwald, pressured by his wife, takes some servants to the King's home and slays the monarch. *Holinshead's Chronicles* also tells of Macbeth and Banquo's meeting with three witches, who make the same prophecies as in Shakespeare's tale. Macbeth and Banquo then plot King Duncan's murder at Lady Macbeth's urging. Shakespeare utilised these storylines, but made changes such as not having Banquo taking part in King Duncan's murder, with Macbeth alone committing this crime. It may be that this particular change was made because it was

believed that Banquo was an actual historical figure that Shakespeare's king, James the First, was descended from, so perhaps it was seen as inappropriate – risky even – to present the monarch's ancestor as a cold-blooded murderer.

Macbeth is full of themes and motifs that run through the play. The main theme is the unchecked lust for power, with Macbeth and his wife, Lady Macbeth, being the main culprits. When Macbeth, a courageous general, is told by one of the Three Witches that he shall be "king hereafter", he is consumed by ambition and, spurred on by Lady Macbeth, he murders King Duncan and assumes the throne for himself. The play shows us how once murder is committed to wrongfully obtain the crown, it often must be committed again and again to maintain power.

Visions and Hallucinations recur throughout the play. As Macbeth and Lady Macbeth commit more murders, their mental state begins to disintegrate, and the audience must wonder whether the visions that appear before them are real or figments of their disturbed imaginations. Just before Macbeth kills Duncan, he sees a bloody dagger floating before him. Later, after the killing of Banquo, he sees, or at least believes he sees, Banquo's ghost sitting in a chair at a feast – a ghost that no one else at the feast notices. Even the cold-blooded Lady Macbeth, perhaps the instigator of these terrible crimes, eventually begins to suffer a breakdown when she sees her hands stained with blood that cannot be washed away.

Witchcraft and prophecy are also motifs that weave themselves through the play. The first scene of the first act, has three witches prophesising that they will next meet together upon a heath where they will meet with Macbeth. Soon after they indeed meet with Macbeth upon a heath, and make a number of prophecies: That Macbeth will become king, that Banquo's heirs will be kings, that Macbeth should "beware Macduff", that Macbeth is safe until Birnam Woods come to Dunsinane, and that "none of woman born / Shall

harm Macbeth". All these prophecies come to pass, with the exception of Banquo's heirs becoming king which presumably happens after the play's conclusion. But were these prophecies self-fulfilling, did they only happen because they were prophesised in the first place?

Macbeth is a fascinating play, and the superstition that runs through the play also, to some extent, runs outside the play itself, with it being considered by some to be bad luck to mention *Macbeth* by name in the theatre. In such cases, actors and others often refer to it as "The Scottish Play" and to the character of Macbeth as "The Scottish King".

One of Shakespeare's most famous and influential plays, in *Macbeth* we see a fascinating discussion on the lust for power, a topic still as potent today as in Shakespeare's time. It is a play that begs many questions: Are the visions in the play real or imagined? Are the witches to blame in large part for the ensuing slaughter, by tempting Macbeth with the crown? Do the witches control Fate or are they merely agents relaying what is bound to happen? Could Lady Macbeth be said to be going against gender stereotypes of the time by being ruthlessly ambitious?

Macbeth is brilliantly intriguing and atmospheric play that has been adapted to film, television, opera and novels, as well as being a favourite in theatres. *Macbeth* has gripped audiences for centuries, and no doubt will continue to be enjoyed by audiences for many generations to come.

David Lear
Editor – Firestone Books

MACBETH

Dramatis Personae

Duncan, King of Scotland

Malcolm and Donalbain – His sons

Macbeth and Banquo – Generals of the King's army

Macduff, Lennox, Ross, Menteith, Angus and Caithness – Noblemen of Scotland

Fleance – Son of Banquo

Siward – Earl of Northumberland, General of the English forces

Young Siward – His son

Seyton – An Officer attending Macbeth

Boy – Son of Macduff

An English Doctor

A Scotch Doctor

A Sergeant

A Porter

An Old Man

Lady Macbeth

Lady Macduff

Gentlewoman attending on Lady Macbeth

Hecate and three witches
Lords, Gentlemen, Officers, Soldiers, Murderers, Attendants and Messengers. The ghost of Banquo, and other Apparitions.

Act I

Scene I. A desert Heath.

[Thunder and lightning. Enter three Witches]

First Witch: When shall we three meet again
In thunder, lightning, or in rain?

Second Witch: When the hurlyburly's done,
When the battle's lost and won.

Third Witch: That will be ere the set of sun.

First Witch: Where the place?

Second Witch: Upon the heath.

Third Witch: There to meet with Macbeth.

First Witch: I come, Graymalkin!

Second Witch: Paddock calls.

Third Witch: Anon.

All: Fair is foul, and foul is fair:
Hover through the fog and filthy air.

[Exeunt]

Scene II. A camp near Forres.

[Alarum within. Enter Duncan, Malcolm,

Donalbain, Lennox, with Attendants, meeting a bleeding Sergeant]

Duncan: What bloody man is that? He can report,
As seemeth by his plight, of the revolt
The newest state.

Malcolm: This is the sergeant
Who like a good and hardy soldier fought
'Gainst my captivity. Hail, brave friend!
Say to the king the knowledge of the broil
As thou didst leave it.

Sergeant: Doubtful it stood;
As two spent swimmers, that do cling together
And choke their art. The merciless Macdonwald-
Worthy to be a rebel, for to that
The multiplying villanies of nature
Do swarm upon him-from the western isles
Of kerns and gallowglasses is supplied;
And fortune, on his damned quarrel smiling,
Show'd like a rebel's whore: but all's too weak:
For brave Macbeth-well he deserves that name-
Disdaining fortune, with his brandish'd steel,
Which smoked with bloody execution,
Like valour's minion carved out his passage

Till he fac'd the slave;
Which ne'er shook hands, nor bade farewell to
him,
Till he unseam'd him from the nave to the chaps,
And fix'd his head upon our battlements.
Duncan: O valiant cousin! worthy gentleman!
Sergeant: As whence the sun 'gins his reflection
Shipwrecking storms and direful thunders break,
So from that spring whence comfort seem'd to
come
Discomfort swells. Mark, king of Scotland, mark:
No sooner justice had with valour arm'd
Compell'd these skipping kerns to trust their heels,
But the Norweyan lord surveying vantage,
With furbish'd arms and new supplies of men
Began a fresh assault.
Duncan: Dismay'd not this
Our captains, Macbeth and Banquo?
Sergeant: Yes;
As sparrows eagles, or the hare the lion.
If I say sooth, I must report they were
As cannons overcharged with double cracks,
So they

Doubly redoubled strokes upon the foe:
Except they meant to bathe in reeking wounds,
Or memorise another Golgotha,
I cannot tell.
But I am faint, my gashes cry for help.

Duncan: So well thy words become thee as thy wounds;
They smack of honour both. Go get him surgeons.
Exit Sergeant, attended
[Enter Ross]
Who comes here?

Malcolm: The worthy thane of Ross.

Lennox: What a haste looks through his eyes! So should he look
That seems to speak things strange.

Ross: God save the king!

Duncan: Whence camest thou, worthy thane?

Ross: From Fife, great king;
Where the Norweyan banners flout the sky
And fan our people cold. Norway himself,
With terrible numbers,
Assisted by that most disloyal traitor
The thane of Cawdor, began a dismal conflict;

Till that Bellona's bridegroom, lapp'd in proof,
Confronted him with self-comparisons,
Point against point, rebellious, arm 'gainst arm.
Curbing his lavish spirit: and, to conclude,
The victory fell on us.
Duncan: Great happiness!
Ross: That now
Sweno, the Norways' king, craves composition:
Nor would we deign him burial of his men
Till he disbursed, at Saint Colme's Inch
Ten thousand dollars to our general use.
Duncan: No more that thane of Cawdor shall deceive
Our bosom interest: go pronounce his present death,
And with his former title greet Macbeth.
Ross: I'll see it done.
Duncan: What he hath lost noble Macbeth hath won.
[Exeunt]

Scene III. A Heath near Forres.

[Thunder. Enter the three Witches.]

First Witch: Where hast thou been, sister?

Second Witch: Killing swine.

Third Witch: Sister, where thou?

First Witch: A sailor's wife had chestnuts in her lap,
And munch'd, and munch'd, and munch'd:-
'Give me,' quoth I:
'Aroint thee, witch!' the rump-fed ronyon cries.
Her husband's to Aleppo gone, master o' the Tiger:
But in a sieve I'll thither sail,
And, like a rat without a tail,
I'll do, I'll do, and I'll do.

Second Witch: I'll give thee a wind.

First Witch: Thou'rt kind.

Third Witch: And I another.

First Witch: I myself have all the other,
And the very ports they blow,
All the quarters that they know
I' the shipman's card.

I will drain him dry as hay:
Sleep shall neither night nor day
Hang upon his pent-house lid;
He shall live a man forbid:
Weary se'nnights nine times nine
Shall he dwindle, peak and pine:
Though his bark cannot be lost,
Yet it shall be tempest-tost.
Look what I have.
Second Witch: Show me, show me.
First Witch: Here I have a pilot's thumb,
Wreck'd as homeward he did come.
[Drum within]
Third Witch: A drum, a drum!
Macbeth doth come.
All: The weird sisters, hand in hand,
Posters of the sea and land,
Thus do go about, about:
Thrice to thine and thrice to mine
And thrice again, to make up nine.
Peace! the charm's wound up.
[Enter Macbeth and Banquo]
Macbeth: So foul and fair a day I have not seen.

Banquo: How far is't call'd to Forres? What are these, so wither'd and so wild in their attire,
That look not like the inhabitants o' the earth,
And yet are on't? Live you? or are you aught
That man may question? You seem to understand me, by each at once her chappy finger laying
Upon her skinny lips: you should be women,
And yet your beards forbid me to interpret
That you are so.

Macbeth: Speak, if you can: what are you?

First Witch: All hail, Macbeth! hail to thee, thane of Glamis!

Second Witch: All hail, Macbeth, hail to thee, thane of Cawdor!

Third Witch: All hail, Macbeth, thou shalt be king hereafter!

Banquo: Good sir, why do you start; and seem to fear
Things that do sound so fair? I' the name of truth,
Are ye fantastical, or that indeed
Which outwardly ye show? My noble partner
You greet with present grace and great prediction
Of noble having and of royal hope,

That he seems rapt withal: to me you speak not.
If you can look into the seeds of time,
And say which grain will grow and which will not,
Speak then to me, who neither beg nor fear
Your favours nor your hate.

First Witch: Hail!

Second Witch: Hail!

Third Witch: Hail!

First Witch: Lesser than Macbeth, and greater.

Second Witch: Not so happy, yet much happier.

Third Witch: Thou shalt get kings, though thou be none:
So all hail, Macbeth and Banquo!

First Witch: Banquo and Macbeth, all hail!

Macbeth: Stay, you imperfect speakers, tell me more:
By Sinel's death I know I am thane of Glamis;
But how of Cawdor? the thane of Cawdor lives,
A prosperous gentleman; and to be king
Stands not within the prospect of belief,
No more than to be Cawdor. Say from whence
You owe this strange intelligence? or why
Upon this blasted heath you stop our way

With such prophetic greeting? Speak, I charge you.

[Witches vanish]

Banquo: The earth hath bubbles, as the water has,

And these are of them. Whither are they vanish'd?

Macbeth: Into the air; and what seem'd corporal melted

As breath into the wind. Would they had stay'd!

Banquo: Were such things here as we do speak about?

Or have we eaten on the insane root

That takes the reason prisoner?

Macbeth: Your children shall be kings.

Banquo: You shall be king.

Macbeth: And thane of Cawdor too: went it not so?

Banquo: To the self-same tune and words. Who's here?

[Enter Ross and Angus]

Ross: The king hath happily received, Macbeth,

The news of thy success; and when he reads

Thy personal venture in the rebels' fight,

His wonders and his praises do contend
Which should be thine or his: silenced with that,
In viewing o'er the rest o' the self-same day,
He finds thee in the stout Norweyan ranks,
Nothing afeard of what thyself didst make,
Strange images of death. As thick as hail
Came post with post; and every one did bear
Thy praises in his kingdom's great defence,
And pour'd them down before him.
Angus: We are sent
To give thee from our royal master thanks;
Only to herald thee into his sight,
Not pay thee.
Ross: And, for an earnest of a greater honour,
He bade me, from him, call thee thane of Cawdor:
In which addition, hail, most worthy thane!
For it is thine.
Banquo: What, can the devil speak true?
Macbeth: The thane of Cawdor lives: why do you dress me
In borrow'd robes?
Angus: Who was the thane lives yet;
But under heavy judgment bears that life

Which he deserves to lose. Whether he was combined
With those of Norway, or did line the rebel
With hidden help and vantage, or that with both
He labour'd in his country's wreck, I know not;
But treasons capital, confess'd and proved,
Have overthrown him.
Macbeth: [Aside] Glamis, and thane of Cawdor!
The greatest is behind. [To Ross and Angus]
Thanks for your pains. [To Banquo] Do you not hope your children shall be kings,
When those that gave the thane of Cawdor to me
Promised no less to them?
Banquo: That trusted home
Might yet enkindle you unto the crown,
Besides the thane of Cawdor. But 'tis strange:
And oftentimes, to win us to our harm,
The instruments of darkness tell us truths,
Win us with honest trifles, to betray's
In deepest consequence.
Cousins, a word, I pray you.
Macbeth: [Aside] Two truths are told,
As happy prologues to the swelling act

Of the imperial theme.-I thank you, gentlemen.
[Aside] This supernatural soliciting
Cannot be ill, cannot be good: if ill,
Why hath it given me earnest of success,
Commencing in a truth? I am thane of Cawdor:
If good, why do I yield to that suggestion
Whose horrid image doth unfix my hair
And make my seated heart knock at my ribs,
Against the use of nature? Present fears
Are less than horrible imaginings:
My thought, whose murder yet is but fantastical,
Shakes so my single state of man that function
Is smother'd in surmise, and nothing is
But what is not.

Banquo: Look, how our partner's rapt.

Macbeth: [Aside] If chance will have me king,
why, chance may crown me,
Without my stir.

Banquo: New honours come upon him,
Like our strange garments, cleave not to their
mould
But with the aid of use.

Macbeth: [Aside] Come what come may,

Time and the hour runs through the roughest day.

Banquo: Worthy Macbeth, we stay upon your leisure.

Macbeth: Give me your favour: my dull brain was wrought
With things forgotten. Kind gentlemen, your pains
Are register'd where every day I turn
The leaf to read them. Let us toward the king.
Think upon what hath chanc'd, and, at more time,
The interim having weigh'd it, let us speak
Our free hearts each to other.

Banquo: Very gladly.

Macbeth: Till then, enough. Come, friends.

[Exeunt]

Scene IV. Forres. A Room in the palace.

[Flourish. Enter Duncan, Malcolm, Donalbain, Lennox, and Attendants]

Duncan: Is execution done on Cawdor? Are not
Those in commission yet return'd?

Malcolm: My liege,
They are not yet come back. But I have spoke

With one that saw him die: who did report
That very frankly he confess'd his treasons,
Implor'd your highness' pardon and set forth
A deep repentance. Nothing in his life
Became him like the leaving it; he died
As one that had been studied in his death
To throw away the dearest thing he ow'd,
As 'twere a careless trifle.
Duncan: There's no art
To find the mind's construction in the face:
He was a gentleman on whom I built
An absolute trust.
[Enter Macbeth, Banquo, Ross, and Angus]
O worthiest cousin!
The sin of my ingratitude even now
Was heavy on me: thou art so far before
That swiftest wing of recompense is slow
To overtake thee. Would thou hadst less deserv'd,
That the proportion both of thanks and payment
Might have been mine! only I have left to say,
More is thy due than more than all can pay.
Macbeth: The service and the loyalty I owe,
In doing it, pays itself. Your highness' part

Is to receive our duties; and our duties
Are to your throne and state, children and servants,
Which do but what they should, by doing every thing
Safe toward your love and honour.

Duncan: Welcome hither:
I have begun to plant thee, and will labour
To make thee full of growing. Noble Banquo,
That hast no less deserved, nor must be known
No less to have done so, let me enfold thee
And hold thee to my heart.

Banquo: There if I grow,
The harvest is your own.

Duncan: My plenteous joys,
Wanton in fulness, seek to hide themselves
In drops of sorrow. Sons, kinsmen, thanes,
And you whose places are the nearest, know
We will establish our estate upon
Our eldest, Malcolm, whom we name hereafter
The Prince of Cumberland; which honour must
Not unaccompanied invest him only,
But signs of nobleness, like stars, shall shine

On all deservers. From hence to Inverness,
And bind us further to you.

Macbeth: The rest is labour, which is not used for you:
I'll be myself the harbinger and make joyful
The hearing of my wife with your approach;
So humbly take my leave.

Duncan: My worthy Cawdor!

Macbeth: [Aside] The Prince of Cumberland! that is a step
On which I must fall down, or else o'er-leap,
For in my way it lies. Stars, hide your fires!
Let not light see my black and deep desires:
The eye wink at the hand; yet let that be,
Which the eye fears, when it is done, to see.
[Exit]

Duncan: True, worthy Banquo; he is full so valiant,
And in his commendations I am fed;
It is a banquet to me. Let's after him,
Whose care is gone before to bid us welcome:
It is a peerless kinsman. [Flourish. Exeunt]

Scene V. Inverness. Macbeth's Castle.

[Enter Lady Macbeth, reading a letter.]

Lady Macbeth: They met me in the day of success: and I have learned by the perfectest report, they have more in them than mortal knowledge. When I burned in desire to question them further, they made themselves air, into which they vanished. Whiles I stood rapt in the wonder of it, came missives from the king, who all-hailed me 'Thane of Cawdor;' by which title, before, these weird sisters saluted me, and referred me to the coming on of time, with 'Hail, king that shalt be!' This have I thought good to deliver thee, my dearest partner of greatness, that thou mightst not lose the dues of rejoicing, by being ignorant of what greatness is promised thee. Lay it to thy heart, and farewell.

Glamis thou art, and Cawdor; and shalt be
What thou art promis'd: yet do I fear thy nature;
It is too full o' the milk of human kindness
To catch the nearest way: thou wouldst be great;
Art not without ambition, but without

The illness should attend it: what thou wouldst highly,
That wouldst thou holily; wouldst not play false,
And yet wouldst wrongly win: thou'ldst have, great Glamis,
That which cries 'Thus thou must do,' if thou have it;
And that which rather thou dost fear to do
Than wishest should be undone. Hie thee hither,
That I may pour my spirits in thine ear;
And chastise with the valour of my tongue
All that impedes thee from the golden round,
Which fate and metaphysical aid doth seem
To have thee crown'd withal.
[Enter a Messenger]
What is your tidings?
Messenger: The king comes here to-night.
Lady Macbeth: Thou'rt mad to say it:
Is not thy master with him? who, were't so,
Would have inform'd for preparation.
Messenger: So please you, it is true: our thane is coming:
One of my fellows had the speed of him,

Who, almost dead for breath, had scarcely more
Than would make up his message.
Lady Macbeth: Give him tending;
He brings great news. [Exit Messenger] The raven himself is hoarse
That croaks the fatal entrance of Duncan
Under my battlements. Come, you spirits
That tend on mortal thoughts, unsex me here,
And fill me from the crown to the toe top-full
Of direst cruelty! make thick my blood;
Stop up the access and passage to remorse,
That no compunctious visitings of nature
Shake my fell purpose, nor keep peace between
The effect and it! Come to my woman's breasts,
And take my milk for gall, you murdering ministers,
Wherever in your sightless substances
You wait on nature's mischief! Come, thick night,
And pall thee in the dunnest smoke of hell,
That my keen knife see not the wound it makes,
Nor heaven peep through the blanket of the dark,
To cry 'Hold, hold!'
[Enter Macbeth]
Great Glamis! worthy Cawdor!

Greater than both, by the all-hail hereafter!
Thy letters have transported me beyond
This ignorant present, and I feel now
The future in the instant.
Macbeth: My dearest love,
Duncan comes here to-night.
Lady Macbeth: And when goes hence?
Macbeth: To-morrow, as he purposes.
Lady Macbeth: O, never
Shall sun that morrow see!
Your face, my thane, is as a book where men
May read strange matters. To beguile the time,
Look like the time; bear welcome in your eye,
Your hand, your tongue: look like the innocent flower,
But be the serpent under't. He that's coming
Must be provided for: and you shall put
This night's great business into my dispatch;
Which shall to all our nights and days to come
Give solely sovereign sway and masterdom.
Macbeth: We will speak further.
Lady Macbeth: Only look up clear;
To alter favour ever is to fear:

Leave all the rest to me.

[Exeunt]

Scene VI. The same. Before the Castle.

[Hautboys and torches. Enter Duncan, Malcolm, Donalbain, Banquo, Lennox, Macduff, Ross, Angus, and Attendants]

Duncan: This castle hath a pleasant seat; the air
Nimbly and sweetly recommends itself
Unto our gentle senses.

Banquo: This guest of summer,
The temple-haunting martlet, does approve,
By his loved mansionry, that the heaven's breath
Smells wooingly here: no jutty, frieze,
Buttress, nor coign of vantage, but this bird
Hath made his pendent bed and procreant cradle:
Where they most breed and haunt, I have observ'd,
The air is delicate.

[Enter Lady Macbeth]

Duncan: See, see, our honour'd hostess!
The love that follows us sometime is our trouble,

Which still we thank as love. Herein I teach you
How you shall bid God 'ild us for your pains,
And thank us for your trouble.

Lady Macbeth: All our service
In every point twice done and then done double
Were poor and single business to contend
Against those honours deep and broad wherewith
Your majesty loads our house: for those of old,
And the late dignities heap'd up to them,
We rest your hermits.

Duncan: Where's the thane of Cawdor?
We cours'd him at the heels, and had a purpose
To be his purveyor: but he rides well;
And his great love, sharp as his spur, hath holp him
To his home before us. Fair and noble hostess,
We are your guest to-night.

Lady Macbeth: Your servants ever
Have theirs, themselves and what is theirs, in compt,
To make their audit at your highness' pleasure,
Still to return your own.

Duncan: Give me your hand;

Conduct me to mine host: we love him highly,
And shall continue our graces towards him.
By your leave, hostess. [Exeunt]

Scene VII. The same. A Room in the Castle.

[Hautboys and torches. Enter and pass over the stage a Sewer, and divers Servants with dishes and service. Then enter Macbeth]

Macbeth: If it were done when 'tis done, then 'twere well
It were done quickly: if the assassination
Could trammel up the consequence, and catch
With his surcease success; that but this blow
Might be the be-all and the end-all here,
But here, upon this bank and shoal of time,
We'ld jump the life to come. But in these cases
We still have judgment here; that we but teach
Bloody instructions, which, being taught, return
To plague the inventor: this even-handed justice
Commends the ingredients of our poison'd chalice
To our own lips. He's here in double trust;
First, as I am his kinsman and his subject,

Strong both against the deed; then, as his host,
Who should against his murderer shut the door,
Not bear the knife myself. Besides, this Duncan
Hath borne his faculties so meek, hath been
So clear in his great office, that his virtues
Will plead like angels, trumpet-tongu'd, against
The deep damnation of his taking-off;
And pity, like a naked new-born babe,
Striding the blast, or heaven's cherubim, hors'd
Upon the sightless couriers of the air,
Shall blow the horrid deed in every eye,
That tears shall drown the wind. I have no spur
To prick the sides of my intent, but only
Vaulting ambition, which o'erleaps itself
And falls on the other.

Enter Lady Macbeth

How now! what news?

Lady Macbeth: He has almost supp'd: why have you left the chamber?

Macbeth: Hath he ask'd for me?

Lady Macbeth: Know you not he has?

Macbeth: We will proceed no further in this business:

He hath honour'd me of late; and I have bought
Golden opinions from all sorts of people,
Which would be worn now in their newest gloss,
Not cast aside so soon.
Lady Macbeth: Was the hope drunk
Wherein you dress'd yourself? hath it slept since?
And wakes it now, to look so green and pale
At what it did so freely? From this time
Such I account thy love. Art thou afeard
To be the same in thine own act and valour
As thou art in desire? Wouldst thou have that
Which thou esteem'st the ornament of life,
And live a coward in thine own esteem,
Letting 'I dare not' wait upon 'I would,'
Like the poor cat i' the adage?
Macbeth: Prithee, peace:
I dare do all that may become a man;
Who dares do more is none.
Lady Macbeth: What beast was't, then,
That made you break this enterprise to me?
When you durst do it, then you were a man;
And, to be more than what you were, you would
Be so much more the man. Nor time nor place

Did then adhere, and yet you would make both:
They have made themselves, and that their fitness now
Does unmake you. I have given suck, and know
How tender 'tis to love the babe that milks me:
I would, while it was smiling in my face,
Have pluck'd my nipple from his boneless gums,
And dash'd the brains out, had I so sworn as you
Have done to this.

Macbeth: If we should fail?

Lady Macbeth: We fail!
But screw your courage to the sticking-place,
And we'll not fail. When Duncan is asleep,
Whereto the rather shall his day's hard journey
Soundly invite him, his two chamberlains
Will I with wine and wassail so convince
That memory, the warder of the brain,
Shall be a fume, and the receipt of reason
A limbeck only: when in swinish sleep
Their drenched natures lie as in a death,
What cannot you and I perform upon
The unguarded Duncan? what not put upon
His spongy officers, who shall bear the guilt

Of our great quell?

Macbeth: Bring forth men-children only;
For thy undaunted mettle should compose
Nothing but males. Will it not be receiv'd,
When we have mark'd with blood those sleepy two
Of his own chamber and us'd their very daggers,
That they have done't?

Lady Macbeth: Who dares receive it other,
As we shall make our griefs and clamour roar
Upon his death?

Macbeth: I am settled, and bend up
Each corporal agent to this terrible feat.
Away, and mock the time with fairest show:
False face must hide what the false heart doth know.

[Exeunt]

Act I: Notes

Act II

Scene I. Inverness. Court within the castle.

[Enter Banquo, and Fleance with a servant bearing a torch before him]

Banquo: How goes the night, boy?

Fleance: The moon is down; I have not heard the clock.

Banquo: And she goes down at twelve.

Fleance: I take't, 'tis later, sir.

Banquo: Hold, take my sword. There's husbandry in heaven;
Their candles are all out. Take thee that too.
A heavy summons lies like lead upon me,
And yet I would not sleep: merciful powers!
Restrain in me the cursed thoughts that nature
Gives way to in repose!
[Enter Macbeth, and a Servant with a torch.]
Give me my sword.
Who's there?

Macbeth: A friend.

Banquo: What, sir, not yet at rest? The king's a-

bed:

He hath been in unusual pleasure, and

Sent forth great largess to your offices.

This diamond he greets your wife withal,

By the name of most kind hostess; and shut up

In measureless content.

Macbeth: Being unprepar'd,

Our will became the servant to defect;

Which else should free have wrought.

Banquo: All's well.

I dreamt last night of the three weird sisters:

To you they have show'd some truth.

Macbeth: I think not of them:

Yet, when we can entreat an hour to serve,

We would spend it in some words upon that business,

If you would grant the time.

Banquo: At your kind'st leisure.

Macbeth: If you shall cleave to my consent, when 'tis,

It shall make honour for you.

Banquo: So I lose none

In seeking to augment it, but still keep

My bosom franchis'd and allegiance clear,
I shall be counsell'd.

Macbeth: Good repose the while!

Banquo: Thanks, sir: the like to you!

[Exeunt Banquo and Fleance]

Macbeth: Go bid thy mistress, when my drink is ready,
She strike upon the bell. Get thee to bed.

[Exit Servant]

Is this a dagger which I see before me,
The handle toward my hand? Come, let me clutch thee.
I have thee not, and yet I see thee still.
Art thou not, fatal vision, sensible
To feeling as to sight? or art thou but
A dagger of the mind, a false creation,
Proceeding from the heat-oppressed brain?
I see thee yet, in form as palpable
As this which now I draw.
Thou marshall'st me the way that I was going;
And such an instrument I was to use.
Mine eyes are made the fools o' the other senses,
Or else worth all the rest; I see thee still,

And on thy blade and dudgeon gouts of blood,
Which was not so before. There's no such thing:
It is the bloody business which informs
Thus to mine eyes. Now o'er the one half-world
Nature seems dead, and wicked dreams abuse
The curtain'd sleep; witchcraft celebrates
Pale Hecate's offerings, and wither'd murder,
Alarum'd by his sentinel, the wolf,
Whose howl's his watch, thus with his stealthy pace.
With Tarquin's ravishing strides, towards his design
Moves like a ghost. Thou sure and firm-set earth,
Hear not my steps, which way they walk, for fear
Thy very stones prate of my whereabout,
And take the present horror from the time,
Which now suits with it. Whiles I threat, he lives:
Words to the heat of deeds too cold breath gives.
[A bell rings]
I go, and it is done; the bell invites me.
Hear it not, Duncan; for it is a knell
That summons thee to heaven or to hell.
[Exit]

Scene II. The same.

[Enter Lady Macbeth]

Lady Macbeth: That which hath made them drunk hath made me bold;
What hath quench'd them hath given me fire.
Hark! Peace!
It was the owl that shriek'd, the fatal bellman,
Which gives the stern'st good-night. He is about it:
The doors are open; and the surfeited grooms
Do mock their charge with snores: I have drugg'd their possets,
That death and nature do contend about them,
Whether they live or die.

Macbeth: [Within] Who's there? what, ho!

Lady Macbeth: Alack, I am afraid they have awaked,
And 'tis not done. The attempt and not the deed
Confounds us. Hark! I laid their daggers ready;
He could not miss them. Had he not resembled
My father as he slept, I had done't.
[Enter Macbeth]
My husband!

Macbeth: I have done the deed. Didst thou not hear a noise?

Lady Macbeth: I heard the owl scream and the crickets cry.

Did not you speak?

Macbeth: When?

Lady Macbeth: Now.

Macbeth: As I descended?

Lady Macbeth: Ay.

Macbeth: Hark!

Who lies i' the second chamber?

Lady Macbeth: Donalbain.

Macbeth: This is a sorry sight.

[Looking on his hands]

Lady Macbeth: A foolish thought, to say a sorry sight.

Macbeth: There's one did laugh in's sleep, and one cried 'Murder!'

That they did wake each other: I stood and heard them:

But they did say their prayers, and address'd them

Again to sleep.

Lady Macbeth: There are two lodged together.

Macbeth: One cried 'God bless us!' and 'Amen' the other;
As they had seen me with these hangman's hands.
Listening their fear, I could not say 'Amen,'
When they did say 'God bless us!'
Lady Macbeth: Consider it not so deeply.
Macbeth: But wherefore could not I pronounce 'Amen'?
I had most need of blessing, and 'Amen'
Stuck in my throat.
Lady Macbeth: These deeds must not be thought
After these ways; so, it will make us mad.
Macbeth: Methought I heard a voice cry 'Sleep no more!
Macbeth does murder sleep', the innocent sleep,
Sleep that knits up the ravell'd sleeve of care,
The death of each day's life, sore labour's bath,
Balm of hurt minds, great nature's second course,
Chief nourisher in life's feast,-
Lady Macbeth: What do you mean?
Macbeth: Still it cried 'Sleep no more!' to all the house:

'Glamis hath murder'd sleep, and therefore
Cawdor
Shall sleep no more; Macbeth shall sleep no
more.'
Lady Macbeth: Who was it that thus cried? Why,
worthy thane,
You do unbend your noble strength, to think
So brainsickly of things. Go get some water,
And wash this filthy witness from your hand.
Why did you bring these daggers from the place?
They must lie there: go carry them; and smear
The sleepy grooms with blood.
Macbeth: I'll go no more:
I am afraid to think what I have done;
Look on't again I dare not.
Lady Macbeth: Infirm of purpose!
Give me the daggers: the sleeping and the dead
Are but as pictures: 'tis the eye of childhood
That fears a painted devil. If he do bleed,
I'll gild the faces of the grooms withal;
For it must seem their guilt. [Exit. Knocking within]
Macbeth: Whence is that knocking?
How is't with me, when every noise appals me?

What hands are here? ha! they pluck out mine eyes.
Will all great Neptune's ocean wash this blood
Clean from my hand? No, this my hand will rather
The multitudinous seas in incarnadine,
Making the green one red.
[Re-enter Lady Macbeth]
Lady Macbeth: My hands are of your colour; but I shame
To wear a heart so white. [Knocking within]
I hear a knocking
At the south entry: retire we to our chamber;
A little water clears us of this deed:
How easy is it, then! Your constancy
Hath left you unattended. [Knocking within]
Hark! more knocking.
Get on your nightgown, lest occasion call us,
And show us to be watchers. Be not lost
So poorly in your thoughts.
Macbeth: To know my deed, 'twere best not know myself. [Knocking within]
Wake Duncan with thy knocking! I would thou couldst! [Exeunt]

Scene III. The same.

[Knocking within. Enter a Porter]

Porter: Here's a knocking indeed! If a man were porter of hell-gate, he should have old turning the key. [Knocking within] Knock, knock, knock! Who's there, i' the name of Beelzebub? Here's a farmer, that hanged himself on the expectation of plenty: come in time; have napkins enow about you; here you'll sweat for't. [Knocking within] Knock, knock! Who's there, in the other devil's name? Faith, here's an equivocator, that could swear in both the scales against either scale; who committed treason enough for God's sake, yet could not equivocate to heaven: O, come in, equivocator. [Knocking within] Knock, knock, knock! Who's there? Faith, here's an English tailor come hither, for stealing out of a French hose: come in, tailor; here you may roast your goose. [Knocking within] Knock, knock; never at quiet! What are you? But this place is too cold for hell. I'll devil-porter

it no further: I had thought to have let in
some of all professions that go the primrose
way to the everlasting bonfire. [Knocking within]
Anon, anon! I pray you, remember the porter.
[Opens the gate]

[Enter Macduff and Lennox]

Macduff: Was it so late, friend, ere you went to
bed,
That you do lie so late?

Porter: 'Faith sir, we were carousing till the second cock: and drink, sir, is a great provoker of three things.

Macduff: What three things does drink especially provoke?

Porter: Marry, sir, nose-painting, sleep, and urine. Lechery, sir, it provokes, and unprovokes; it provokes the desire, but it takes away the performance: therefore, much drink may be said to be an equivocator with lechery: it makes him, and it mars him; it sets him on, and it takes him off; it persuades him, and disheartens him; makes him stand to, and not stand to; in conclusion, equivocates him in a sleep, and, giving him the lie,

leaves him.

Macduff: I believe drink gave thee the lie last night.

Porter: That it did, sir, i' the very throat on me: but I requited him for his lie; and, I think, being too strong for him, though he took up my legs sometime, yet I made a shift to cast him.

Macduff: Is thy master stirring?

[Enter Macbeth]

Our knocking has awak'd him; here he comes.

Lennox: Good morrow, noble sir.

Macbeth: Good morrow, both.

Macduff: Is the king stirring, worthy thane?

Macbeth: Not yet.

Macduff: He did command me to call timely on him:

I have almost slipp'd the hour.

Macbeth: I'll bring you to him.

Macduff: I know this is a joyful trouble to you;

But yet 'tis one.

Macbeth: The labour we delight in physics pain.

This is the door.

Macduff: I'll make so bold to call,

For 'tis my limited service.

[Exit]

Lennox: Goes the king hence to-day?

Macbeth: He does: he did appoint so.

Lennox: The night has been unruly: where we lay,
Our chimneys were blown down; and, as they say,
Lamentings heard i' the air; strange screams of death,
And prophesying with accents terrible
Of dire combustion and confus'd events
New hatch'd to the woeful time: the obscure bird
Clamour'd the livelong night: some say, the earth
Was feverous and did shake.

Macbeth: 'Twas a rough night.

Lennox: My young remembrance cannot parallel
A fellow to it.

[Re-enter Macduff]

Macduff: O horror, horror, horror! Tongue nor heart
Cannot conceive nor name thee!

Macbeth and **Lennox:** What's the matter?

Macduff: Confusion now hath made his masterpiece!

Most sacrilegious murder hath broke ope
The Lord's anointed temple, and stole thence
The life o' the building!

Macbeth: What is 't you say? the life?

Lennox: Mean you his majesty?

Macduff: Approach the chamber, and destroy
your sight
With a new Gorgon: do not bid me speak;
See, and then speak yourselves.
[Exeunt Macbeth and Lennox]
Awake, awake!
Ring the alarum-bell. Murder and treason!
Banquo and Donalbain! Malcolm! awake!
Shake off this downy sleep, death's counterfeit,
And look on death itself! up, up, and see
The great doom's image! Malcolm! Banquo!
As from your graves rise up, and walk like sprites,
To countenance this horror! Ring the bell.
[Bell rings]
[Enter Lady Macbeth]

Lady Macbeth: What's the business,
That such a hideous trumpet calls to parley
The sleepers of the house? speak, speak!

Macduff: O gentle lady,

'Tis not for you to hear what I can speak:

The repetition, in a woman's ear,

Would murder as it fell.

[Enter Banquo]

O Banquo, Banquo,

Our royal master 's murder'd!

Lady Macbeth: Woe, alas!

What, in our house?

Banquo: Too cruel any where.

Dear Duff, I prithee, contradict thyself,

And say it is not so.

[Re-enter Malcolm and Lennox, with Ross]

Macbeth: Had I but died an hour before this chance,

I had liv'd a blessed time; for, from this instant,

There 's nothing serious in mortality:

All is but toys: renown and grace is dead;

The wine of life is drawn, and the mere lees

Is left this vault to brag of.

[Enter Malcolm and Donalbain]

Donalbain: What is amiss?

Macbeth: You are, and do not know't:

The spring, the head, the fountain of your blood
Is stopp'd; the very source of it is stopp'd.

Macduff: Your royal father 's murder'd.

Malcolm: O, by whom?

Lennox: Those of his chamber, as it seem'd, had done 't:
Their hands and faces were an badged with blood;
So were their daggers, which unwiped we found
Upon their pillows:
They stared, and were distracted; no man's life
Was to be trusted with them.

Macbeth: O, yet I do repent me of my fury,
That I did kill them.

Macduff: Wherefore did you so?

Macbeth: Who can be wise, amazed, temperate and furious,
Loyal and neutral, in a moment? No man:
The expedition my violent love
Outrun the pauser, reason. Here lay Duncan,
His silver skin laced with his golden blood;
And his gash'd stabs look'd like a breach in nature
For ruin's wasteful entrance: there, the murderers,
Steep'd in the colours of their trade, their daggers

Unmannerly breech'd with gore: who could refrain,
That had a heart to love, and in that heart
Courage to make 's love known?

Lady Macbeth: Help me hence, ho!

Macduff: Look to the lady.

Malcolm: [Aside to Donalbain] Why do we hold our tongues,
That most may claim this argument for ours?

Donalbain: [Aside to Malcolm] What should be spoken here, where our fate,
Hid in an auger-hole, may rush, and seize us?
Let 's away; our tears are not yet brew'd.

Malcolm: [Aside to Donalbain] Nor our strong sorrow
Upon the foot of motion.

Banquo: Look to the lady:
[Lady Macbeth is carried out]
And when we have our naked frailties hid,
That suffer in exposure, let us meet,
And question this most bloody piece of work,
To know it further. Fears and scruples shake us:
In the great hand of God I stand; and thence
Against the undivulged pretence I fight

Of treasonous malice.

Macduff: And so do I.

All: So all.

Macbeth: Let's briefly put on manly readiness,

And meet i' the hall together.

All: Well contented.

Exeunt all but Malcolm and Donalbain.

Malcolm: What will you do? Let's not consort with them:

To show an unfelt sorrow is an office

Which the false man does easy. I'll to England.

Donalbain: To Ireland, I; our separated fortune

Shall keep us both the safer: where we are,

There's daggers in men's smiles: the near in blood,

The nearer bloody.

Malcolm: This murderous shaft that's shot

Hath not yet lighted, and our safest way

Is to avoid the aim. Therefore, to horse;

And let us not be dainty of leave-taking,

But shift away: there's warrant in that theft

Which steals itself, when there's no mercy left.

[Exeunt]

Scene IV. The Same. Without the Castle.

[Enter Ross and an Old Man]

Old Man: Threescore and ten I can remember well:
Within the volume of which time I have seen
Hours dreadful and things strange; but this sore night
Hath trifled former knowings.

Ross: Ah, good father,
Thou seest, the heavens, as troubled with man's act,
Threaten his bloody stage: by the clock, 'tis day,
And yet dark night strangles the travelling lamp:
Is't night's predominance, or the day's shame,
That darkness does the face of earth entomb,
When living light should kiss it?

Old Man: 'Tis unnatural,
Even like the deed that's done. On Tuesday last,
A falcon, towering in her pride of place,
Was by a mousing owl hawk'd at and kill'd.

Ross: And Duncan's horses-a thing most strange and certain-

Beauteous and swift, the minions of their race,

Turn'd wild in nature, broke their stalls, flung out,

Contending 'gainst obedience, as they would make

War with mankind.

Old Man: 'Tis said they eat each other.

Ross: They did so, to the amazement of mine eyes

That look'd upon't. Here comes the good Macduff.

[Enter Macduff]

How goes the world, sir, now?

Macduff: Why, see you not?

Ross: Is't known who did this more than bloody deed?

Macduff: Those that Macbeth hath slain.

Ross: Alas, the day!

What good could they pretend?

Macduff: They were suborn'd:

Malcolm and Donalbain, the king's two sons,

Are stol'n away and fled; which puts upon them

Suspicion of the deed.

Ross: 'Gainst nature still!

Thriftless ambition, that wilt ravin up

Thine own life's means! Then 'tis most like

The sovereignty will fall upon Macbeth.

Macduff: He is already named, and gone to Scone

To be invested.

Ross: Where is Duncan's body?

Macduff: Carried to Colmekill,

The sacred storehouse of his predecessors,

And guardian of their bones.

Ross: Will you to Scone?

Macduff: No, cousin, I'll to Fife.

Ross: Well, I will thither.

Macduff: Well, may you see things well done there: adieu!

Lest our old robes sit easier than our new!

Ross: Farewell, father.

Old Man: God's benison go with you; and with those

That would make good of bad, and friends of foes!

[Exeunt]

Act II: Notes

Act III

Scene I. Forres. A Room in the Palace.

[Enter Banquo]

Banquo: Thou hast it now: king, Cawdor, Glamis, all,

As the weird women promised, and, I fear,

Thou play'dst most foully for't: yet it was said

It should not stand in thy posterity,

But that myself should be the root and father

Of many kings. If there come truth from them-

As upon thee, Macbeth, their speeches shine-

Why, by the verities on thee made good,

May they not be my oracles as well,

And set me up in hope? But hush! no more.

[Sennet sounded. Enter Macbeth, as king, Lady Macbeth, as queen, Lennox, Ross, Lords, Ladies, and Attendants]

Macbeth: Here's our chief guest.

Lady Macbeth: If he had been forgotten,

It had been as a gap in our great feast,

And all-thing unbecoming.

Macbeth: To-night we hold a solemn supper, sir,
And I'll request your presence.
Banquo: Let your highness
Command upon me; to the which my duties
Are with a most indissoluble tie
For ever knit.
Macbeth: Ride you this afternoon?
Banquo: Ay, my good lord.
Macbeth: We should have else desir'd your good advice,
Which still hath been both grave and prosperous,
In this day's council; but we'll take to-morrow.
Is't far you ride?
Banquo: As far, my lord, as will fill up the time
'Twixt this and supper: go not my horse the better,
I must become a borrower of the night
For a dark hour or twain.
Macbeth: Fail not our feast.
Banquo: My lord, I will not.
Macbeth: We hear, our bloody cousins are bestow'd
In England and in Ireland, not confessing
Their cruel parricide, filling their hearers

With strange invention: but of that to-morrow,
When therewithal we shall have cause of state
Craving us jointly. Hie you to horse: adieu,
Till you return at night. Goes Fleance with you?

Banquo: Ay, my good lord: our time does call upon 's.

Macbeth: I wish your horses swift and sure of foot;
And so I do commend you to their backs. Farewell.

[Exit Banquo]

Let every man be master of his time
Till seven at night: to make society
The sweeter welcome, we will keep ourself
Till supper-time alone: while then, God be with you!

[Exeunt all but Macbeth, and an Attendant]

Sirrah, a word with you: attend those men
Our pleasure?

Attendant: They are, my lord, without the palace gate.

Macbeth: Bring them before us.

[Exit Attendant]

To be thus is nothing;
But to be safely thus.-Our fears in Banquo

Stick deep; and in his royalty of nature
Reigns that which would be fear'd: 'tis much he dares;
And, to that dauntless temper of his mind,
He hath a wisdom that doth guide his valour
To act in safety. There is none but he
Whose being I do fear: and, under him,
My Genius is rebuk'd; as, it is said,
Mark Antony's was by Caesar. He chid the sisters
When first they put the name of king upon me,
And bade them speak to him: then prophet-like
They hail'd him father to a line of kings:
Upon my head they placed a fruitless crown,
And put a barren sceptre in my gripe,
Thence to be wrench'd with an unlineal hand,
No son of mine succeeding. If 't be so,
For Banquo's issue have I fil'd my mind;
For them the gracious Duncan have I murder'd;
Put rancours in the vessel of my peace
Only for them; and mine eternal jewel
Given to the common enemy of man,
To make them kings, the seed of Banquo kings!
Rather than so, come fate into the list.

And champion me to the utterance! Who's there!

[Re-enter Attendant, with two Murderers]

Now go to the door, and stay there till we call.

[Exit Attendant]

Was it not yesterday we spoke together?

First Murderer: It was, so please your highness.

Macbeth: Well then, now

Have you consider'd of my speeches? Know

That it was he in the times past which held you

So under fortune, which you thought had been

Our innocent self: this I made good to you

In our last conference, pass'd in probation with you,

How you were borne in hand, how cross'd, the instruments,

Who wrought with them, and all things else that might

To half a soul and to a notion crazed

Say 'Thus did Banquo.'

First Murderer: You made it known to us.

Macbeth: I did so, and went further, which is now

Our point of second meeting. Do you find

Your patience so predominant in your nature

That you can let this go? Are you so gospell'd
To pray for this good man and for his issue,
Whose heavy hand hath bow'd you to the grave
And beggar'd yours for ever?
First Murderer: We are men, my liege.
Macbeth: Ay, in the catalogue ye go for men;
As hounds and greyhounds, mongrels, spaniels, curs,
Shoughs, water-rugs and demi-wolves, are clept
All by the name of dogs: the valued file
Distinguishes the swift, the slow, the subtle,
The housekeeper, the hunter, every one
According to the gift which bounteous nature
Hath in him closed; whereby he does receive
Particular addition. from the bill
That writes them all alike: and so of men.
Now, if you have a station in the file,
Not i' the worst rank of manhood, say 't;
And I will put that business in your bosoms,
Whose execution takes your enemy off,
Grapples you to the heart and love of us,
Who wear our health but sickly in his life,
Which in his death were perfect.

Second Murderer: I am one, my liege,
Whom the vile blows and buffets of the world
Have so incensed that I am reckless what
I do to spite the world.
First Murderer: And I another
So weary with disasters, tugg'd with fortune,
That I would set my lie on any chance,
To mend it, or be rid on't.
Macbeth: Both of you
Know Banquo was your enemy.
Both Murderers: True, my lord.
Macbeth: So is he mine; and in such bloody distance,
That every minute of his being thrusts
Against my near'st of life: and though I could
With bare-fac'd power sweep him from my sight
And bid my will avouch it, yet I must not,
For certain friends that are both his and mine,
Whose loves I may not drop, but wail his fall
Who I myself struck down; and thence it is,
That I to your assistance do make love,
Masking the business from the common eye
For sundry weighty reasons.

Second Murderer: We shall, my lord,

Perform what you command us.

First Murderer: Though our lives-

Macbeth: Your spirits shine through you. Within this hour at most

I will advise you where to plant yourselves;

Acquaint you with the perfect spy o' the time,

The moment on't; for't must be done to-night,

And something from the palace; always thought

That I require a clearness: and with him-

To leave no rubs nor botches in the work-

Fleance his son, that keeps him company,

Whose absence is no less material to me

Than is his father's, must embrace the fate

Of that dark hour. Resolve yourselves apart:

I'll come to you anon.

Both Murderers: We are resolved, my lord.

Macbeth: I'll call upon you straight: abide within.

[Exeunt Murderers]

It is concluded. Banquo, thy soul's flight,

If it find heaven, must find it out to-night.

[Exit]

Scene II. The palace.

[Enter Lady Macbeth and a Servant]

Lady Macbeth: Is Banquo gone from court?

Servant: Ay, madam, but returns again to-night.

Lady Macbeth: Say to the king, I would attend his leisure

For a few words.

Servant: Madam, I will.

[Exit]

Lady Macbeth: Nought's had, all's spent,

Where our desire is got without content:

'Tis safer to be that which we destroy

Than by destruction dwell in doubtful joy.

[Enter Macbeth]

How now, my lord! why do you keep alone,

Of sorriest fancies your companions making,

Using those thoughts which should indeed have died

With them they think on? Things without all remedy

Should be without regard: what's done is done.

Macbeth: We have scotch'd the snake, not kill'd it:

She'll close and be herself, whilst our poor malice
Remains in danger of her former tooth.
But let the frame of things disjoint, both the
worlds suffer,
Ere we will eat our meal in fear and sleep
In the affliction of these terrible dreams
That shake us nightly: better be with the dead,
Whom we, to gain our peace, have sent to peace,
Than on the torture of the mind to lie
In restless ecstasy. Duncan is in his grave;
After life's fitful fever he sleeps well;
Treason has done his worst: nor steel, nor poison,
Malice domestic, foreign levy, nothing,
Can touch him further.
Lady Macbeth: Come on;
Gentle my lord, sleek o'er your rugged looks;
Be bright and jovial among your guests to-night.
Macbeth: So shall I, love; and so, I pray, be you:
Let your remembrance apply to Banquo;
Present him eminence, both with eye and tongue:
Unsafe the while, that we
Must lave our honours in these flattering streams,
And make our faces vizards to our hearts,

Disguising what they are.

Lady Macbeth: You must leave this.

Macbeth: O, full of scorpions is my mind, dear wife!

Thou know'st that Banquo, and his Fleance, lives.

Lady Macbeth: But in them nature's copy's not eterne.

Macbeth: There's comfort yet; they are assailable;

Then be thou jocund: ere the bat hath flown

His cloister'd flight, ere to black Hecate's summons

The shard-borne beetle with his drowsy hums

Hath rung night's yawning peal, there shall be done

A deed of dreadful note.

Lady Macbeth: What's to be done?

Macbeth: Be innocent of the knowledge, dearest chuck,

Till thou applaud the deed. Come, seeling night,

Scarf up the tender eye of pitiful day;

And with thy bloody and invisible hand

Cancel and tear to pieces that great bond

Which keeps me pale! Light thickens; and the crow

Makes wing to the rooky wood:

Good things of day begin to droop and drowse;
While night's black agents to their preys do rouse.
Thou marvell'st at my words: but hold thee still;
Things bad begun make strong themselves by ill.
So, prithee, go with me.
[Exeunt]

Scene III. The Same. A park with a Road leading to the Palace.

[Enter three Murderers]
First Murderer: But who did bid thee join with us?
Third Murderer: Macbeth.
Second Murderer: He needs not our mistrust, since he delivers
Our offices and what we have to do
To the direction just.
First Murderer: Then stand with us.
The west yet glimmers with some streaks of day:
Now spurs the lated traveller apace
To gain the timely inn; and near approaches
The subject of our watch.
Third Murderer: Hark! I hear horses.

Banquo: [Within] Give us a light there, ho!

Second Murderer: Then 'tis he: the rest
That are within the note of expectation
Already are i' the court.

First Murderer: His horses go about.

Third Murderer: Almost a mile: but he does usually,
So all men do, from hence to the palace gate
Make it their walk.

Second Murderer: A light, a light!

[Enter Banquo, and Fleance with a torch]

Third Murderer: 'Tis he.

First Murderer: Stand to't.

Banquo: It will be rain to-night.

First Murderer: Let it come down.

[They set upon Banquo]

Banquo: O, treachery! Fly, good Fleance, fly, fly, fly!
Thou mayst revenge. O slave!

[Dies. Fleance escapes]

Third Murderer: Who did strike out the light?

First Murderer: Wast not the way?

Third Murderer: There's but one down; the son is

fled.

Second Murderer: We have lost

Best half of our affair.

First Murderer: Well, let's away, and say how much is done.

[Exeunt]

Scene IV. The same. A Room of State in the Palace.

[A banquet prepared. Enter Macbeth, Lady Macbeth, Ross, Lennox, Lords, and Attendants]

Macbeth: You know your own degrees; sit down: at first

And last the hearty welcome.

Lords: Thanks to your majesty.

Macbeth: Ourself will mingle with society,

And play the humble host.

Our hostess keeps her state, but in best time

We will require her welcome.

Lady Macbeth: Pronounce it for me, sir, to all our friends;

For my heart speaks they are welcome.

[First Murderer appears at the door]

Macbeth: See, they encounter thee with their hearts' thanks.
Both sides are even: here I'll sit i' the midst:
Be large in mirth; anon we'll drink a measure
The table round. [Approaching the door] There's blood on thy face.

First Murderer: 'Tis Banquo's then.

Macbeth: 'Tis better thee without than he within.
Is he dispatch'd?

First Murderer: My lord, his throat is cut; that I did for him.

Macbeth: Thou art the best o' the cut-throats: yet he's good
That did the like for Fleance: if thou didst it,
Thou art the nonpareil.

First Murderer: Most royal sir,
Fleance is 'scaped.

Macbeth: Then comes my fit again: I had else been perfect,
Whole as the marble, founded as the rock,
As broad and general as the casing air:
But now I am cabin'd, cribb'd, confined, bound in

To saucy doubts and fears. But Banquo's safe?

First Murderer: Ay, my good lord: safe in a ditch he bides,

With twenty trenched gashes on his head;

The least a death to nature.

Macbeth: Thanks for that:

There the grown serpent lies; the worm that's fled

Hath nature that in time will venom breed,

No teeth for the present. Get thee gone: to-morrow

We'll hear, ourselves, again.

[Exit Murderer]

Lady Macbeth: My royal lord,

You do not give the cheer: the feast is sold

That is not often vouch'd, while 'tis a-making,

'Tis given with welcome: to feed were best at home;

From thence the sauce to meat is ceremony;

Meeting were bare without it.

Macbeth: Sweet remembrancer!

Now, good digestion wait on appetite,

And health on both!

Lennox: May't please your highness sit.

[The Ghost of Banquo enters, and sits in Macbeth's

place]

Macbeth: Here had we now our country's honour roof'd,

Were the graced person of our Banquo present;

Who may I rather challenge for unkindness

Than pity for mischance!

Ross: His absence, sir,

Lays blame upon his promise. Please't your highness

To grace us with your royal company.

Macbeth: The table's full.

Lennox: Here is a place reserved, sir.

Macbeth: Where?

Lennox: Here, my good lord. What is't that moves your highness?

Macbeth: Which of you have done this?

Lords: What, my good lord?

Macbeth: Thou canst not say I did it: never shake

Thy gory locks at me.

Ross: Gentlemen, rise: his highness is not well.

Lady Macbeth: Sit, worthy friends: my lord is often thus,

And hath been from his youth: pray you, keep

seat;
The fit is momentary; upon a thought
He will again be well: if much you note him,
You shall offend him and extend his passion:
Feed, and regard him not. Are you a man?

Macbeth: Ay, and a bold one, that dare look on that
Which might appal the devil.

Lady Macbeth: O proper stuff!
This is the very painting of your fear:
This is the air-drawn dagger which, you said,
Led you to Duncan. O, these flaws and starts,
Impostors to true fear, would well become
A woman's story at a winter's fire,
Authoriz'd by her grandam. Shame itself!
Why do you make such faces? When all's done,
You look but on a stool.

Macbeth: Prithee, see there! behold! look! lo! how say you?
Why, what care I? If thou canst nod, speak too.
If charnel-houses and our graves must send
Those that we bury back, our monuments
Shall be the maws of kites.

[Ghost disappears]

Lady Macbeth: What, quite unmann'd in folly?

Macbeth: If I stand here, I saw him.

Lady Macbeth: Fie, for shame!

Macbeth: Blood hath been shed ere now, i' the olden time,
Ere human statute purg'd the gentle weal;
Ay, and since too, murders have been perform'd
Too terrible for the ear: the times have been,
That, when the brains were out, the man would die,
And there an end; but now they rise again,
With twenty mortal murders on their crowns,
And push us from our stools: this is more strange
Than such a murder is.

Lady Macbeth: My worthy lord,
Your noble friends do lack you.

Macbeth: I do forget.
Do not muse at me, my most worthy friends,
I have a strange infirmity, which is nothing
To those that know me. Come, love and health to all;
Then I'll sit down. Give me some wine; fill full.

I drink to the general joy o' the whole table,
And to our dear friend Banquo, whom we miss;
Would he were here! to all, and him, we thirst,
And all to all.

Lords: Our duties, and the pledge.

[Re-enter Ghost]

Macbeth: Avaunt! and quit my sight! let the earth hide thee!
Thy bones are marrowless, thy blood is cold;
Thou hast no speculation in those eyes
Which thou dost glare with!

Lady Macbeth: Think of this, good peers,
But as a thing of custom: 'tis no other;
Only it spoils the pleasure of the time.

Macbeth: What man dare, I dare:
Approach thou like the rugged Russian bear,
The arm'd rhinoceros, or the Hyrcan tiger;
Take any shape but that, and my firm nerves
Shall never tremble: or be alive again,
And dare me to the desert with thy sword;
If trembling I inhabit then, protest me
The baby of a girl. Hence, horrible shadow!
Unreal mockery, hence!

[Ghost vanishes]

Why, so: being gone,

I am a man again. Pray you, sit still.

Lady Macbeth: You have displaced the mirth, broke the good meeting,

With most admir'd disorder.

Macbeth: Can such things be,

And overcome us like a summer's cloud,

Without our special wonder? You make me strange

Even to the disposition that I owe,

When now I think you can behold such sights,

And keep the natural ruby of your cheeks,

When mine is blanched with fear.

Ross: What sights, my lord?

Lady Macbeth: I pray you, speak not; he grows worse and worse;

Question enrages him. At once, good-night:

Stand not upon the order of your going,

But go at once.

Lennox: Good-night; and better health

Attend his majesty!

Lady Macbeth: A kind good night to all!

[Exeunt Lords and Attendants]

Macbeth: It will have blood; they say, blood will have blood:

Stones have been known to move and trees to speak;

Augurs and understood relations have

By maggot-pies and choughs and rooks brought forth

The secret'st man of blood. What is the night?

Lady Macbeth: Almost at odds with morning, which is which.

Macbeth: How say'st thou, that Macduff denies his person

At our great bidding?

Lady Macbeth: Did you send to him, sir?

Macbeth: I hear it by the way; but I will send:

There's not a one of them but in his house

I keep a servant fee'd. I will to-morrow,

And betimes I will, to the weird sisters:

More shall they speak; for now I am bent to know,

By the worst means, the worst. For mine own good,

All causes shall give way: I am in blood

Stepp'd in so far that, should I wade no more,
Returning were as tedious as go o'er:
Strange things I have in head, that will to hand;
Which must be acted ere they may be scann'd.

Lady Macbeth: You lack the season of all natures, sleep.

Macbeth: Come, we'll to sleep. My strange and self-abuse
Is the initiate fear that wants hard use:
We are yet but young in deed.
[Exeunt]

Scene V. A Heath.

[Thunder. Enter the three Witches meeting Hecate]

First Witch: Why, how now, Hecate! you look angerly.

Hecate: Have I not reason, beldams as you are,
Saucy and overbold? How did you dare
To trade and traffic with Macbeth
In riddles and affairs of death;
And I, the mistress of your charms,

The close contriver of all harms,
Was never call'd to bear my part,
Or show the glory of our art?
And, which is worse, all you have done
Hath been but for a wayward son,
Spiteful and wrathful, who, as others do,
Loves for his own ends, not for you.
But make amends now: get you gone,
And at the pit of Acheron
Meet me i' the morning: thither he
Will come to know his destiny:
Your vessels and your spells provide,
Your charms and every thing beside.
I am for the air; this night I'll spend
Unto a dismal and a fatal end:
Great business must be wrought ere noon:
Upon the corner of the moon
There hangs a vaporous drop profound;
I'll catch it ere it come to ground:
And that distill'd by magic sleights
Shall raise such artificial sprites
As by the strength of their illusion
Shall draw him on to his confusion:

He shall spurn fate, scorn death, and bear
He hopes 'bove wisdom, grace and fear:
And you all know, security
Is mortals' chiefest enemy.
Music and a song within: 'Come away, come away,' & c
Hark! I am call'd; my little spirit, see,
Sits in a foggy cloud, and stays for me.
[Exit]

First Witch: Come, let's make haste; she'll soon be back again.

[Exeunt]

Scene VI. Forres. A Room in the Palace.

[Enter Lennox and another Lord.]

Lennox: My former speeches have but hit your thoughts,
Which can interpret further: only, I say,
Things have been strangely borne. The gracious Duncan
Was pitied of Macbeth: marry, he was dead:
And the right-valiant Banquo walk'd too late;

Whom, you may say, if't please you, Fleance kill'd,
For Fleance fled: men must not walk too late.
Who cannot want the thought how monstrous
It was for Malcolm and for Donalbain
To kill their gracious father? damned fact!
How it did grieve Macbeth! did he not straight
In pious rage the two delinquents tear,
That were the slaves of drink and thralls of sleep?
Was not that nobly done? Ay, and wisely too;
For 'twould have anger'd any heart alive
To hear the men deny't. So that, I say,
He has borne all things well: and I do think
That had he Duncan's sons under his key-
As, an't please heaven, he shall not-they should find
What 'twere to kill a father; so should Fleance.
But, peace! for from broad words and 'cause he fail'd
His presence at the tyrant's feast, I hear
Macduff lives in disgrace. Sir, can you tell
Where he bestows himself?
Lord: The son of Duncan,
From whom this tyrant holds the due of birth

Lives in the English court, and is receiv'd
Of the most pious Edward with such grace
That the malevolence of fortune nothing
Takes from his high respect: thither Macduff
Is gone to pray the holy king, upon his aid
To wake Northumberland and war-like Siward:
That, by the help of these-with Him above
To ratify the work-we may again
Give to our tables meat, sleep to our nights,
Free from our feasts and banquets bloody knives,
Do faithful homage and receive free honours:
All which we pine for now: and this report
Hath so exasperate the king that he
Prepares for some attempt of war.
Lennox: Sent he to Macduff?
Lord: He did: and with an absolute 'Sir, not I,'
The cloudy messenger turns me his back,
And hums, as who should say 'You'll rue the time
That clogs me with this answer.'
Lennox: And that well might
Advise him to a caution, to hold what distance
His wisdom can provide. Some holy angel
Fly to the court of England and unfold

His message ere he come, that a swift blessing

May soon return to this our suffering country

Under a hand accursed!

Lord: I'll send my prayers with him.

[Exeunt]

Act III: Notes

Act IV

Scene I. A Cavern. In the middle, a boiling Cauldron.

[Thunder. Enter the three Witches]

First Witch: Thrice the brinded cat hath mew'd.

Second Witch: Thrice and once the hedge-pig whined.

Third Witch: Harpier cries 'Tis time, 'tis time.

First Witch: Round about the cauldron go;
In the poison'd entrails throw.
Toad, that under cold stone
Days and nights has thirty-one
Swelter'd venom sleeping got,
Boil thou first i' the charmed pot.

All: Double, double toil and trouble;
Fire burn, and cauldron bubble.

Second Witch: Fillet of a fenny snake,
In the cauldron boil and bake;
Eye of newt and toe of frog,
Wool of bat and tongue of dog,
Adder's fork and blind-worm's sting,

Lizard's leg and owlet's wing,
For a charm of powerful trouble,
Like a hell-broth boil and bubble.
ALL: Double, double toil and trouble;
Fire burn and cauldron bubble.
Third Witch: Scale of dragon, tooth of wolf,
Witches' mummy, maw and gulf
Of the ravin'd salt-sea shark,
Root of hemlock digg'd i' the dark,
Liver of blaspheming Jew,
Gall of goat, and slips of yew
Silver'd in the moon's eclipse,
Nose of Turk and Tartar's lips,
Finger of birth-strangled babe
Ditch-deliver'd by a drab,
Make the gruel thick and slab:
Add thereto a tiger's chaudron,
For the ingredients of our cauldron.
All: Double, double toil and trouble;
Fire burn and cauldron bubble.
Second Witch: Cool it with a baboon's blood,
Then the charm is firm and good.
[Enter Hecate to the other three Witches]

Hecate: O, well done! I commend your pains;

And every one shall share i' the gains;

And now about the cauldron sing,

Like elves and fairies in a ring,

Enchanting all that you put in.

[Music and a song: 'Black spirits,' etc]

[Hecate retires]

Second Witch: By the pricking of my thumbs,

Something wicked this way comes.

Open, locks,

Whoever knocks!

[Enter Macbeth]

Macbeth: How now, you secret, black, and midnight hags!

What is't you do?

All: A deed without a name.

Macbeth: I conjure you, by that which you profess,

Howe'er you come to know it, answer me:

Though you untie the winds and let them fight

Against the churches; though the yesty waves

Confound and swallow navigation up;

Though bladed corn be lodged and trees blown down;

Though castles topple on their warders' heads;
Though palaces and pyramids do slope
Their heads to their foundations; though the treasure
Of nature's germens tumble all together,
Even till destruction sicken; answer me
To what I ask you.

First Witch: Speak.

Second Witch: Demand.

Third Witch: We'll answer.

First Witch: Say, if thou'dst rather hear it from our mouths,
Or from our masters'?

Macbeth: Call 'em; let me see 'em.

First Witch: Pour in sow's blood, that hath eaten
Her nine farrow; grease that's sweaten
From the murderer's gibbet throw
Into the flame.

All: Come, high or low;
Thyself and office deftly show!

[Thunder. First Apparition: an armed Head]

Macbeth: Tell me, thou unknown power,-

First Witch: He knows thy thought:

Hear his speech, but say thou nought.

First Apparition: Macbeth! Macbeth! Macbeth!

beware Macduff;

Beware the thane of Fife. Dismiss me. Enough.

[Descends]

Macbeth: Whate'er thou art, for thy good caution,

thanks;

Thou hast harp'd my fear aright: but one

word more,-

First Witch: He will not be commanded: here's

another,

More potent than the first.

[Thunder. Second Apparition: A bloody Child]

Second Apparition: Macbeth! Macbeth! Macbeth!

Macbeth: Had I three ears, I'ld hear thee.

Second Apparition: Be bloody, bold, and

resolute; laugh to scorn

The power of man, for none of woman born

Shall harm Macbeth.

[Descends]

Macbeth: Then live, Macduff: what need I fear of

thee?

But yet I'll make assurance double sure,

And take a bond of fate: thou shalt not live;
That I may tell pale-hearted fear it lies,
And sleep in spite of thunder.
[Thunder. Third Apparition: a Child crowned, with a tree in his hand]
What is this
That rises like the issue of a king,
And wears upon his baby-brow the round
And top of sovereignty?

All: Listen, but speak not to't.

Third Apparition: Be lion-mettled, proud; and take no care
Who chafes, who frets, or where conspirers are:
Macbeth shall never vanquish'd be until
Great Birnam wood to high Dunsinane hill
Shall come against him.
[Descends]

Macbeth: That will never be
Who can impress the forest, bid the tree
Unfix his earth-bound root? Sweet bodements! good!
Rebellion's head, rise never till the wood
Of Birnam rise, and our high-placed Macbeth

Shall live the lease of nature, pay his breath
To time and mortal custom. Yet my heart
Throbs to know one thing: tell me, if your art
Can tell so much: shall Banquo's issue ever
Reign in this kingdom?

All: Seek to know no more.

Macbeth: I will be satisfied: deny me this,
And an eternal curse fall on you! Let me know.
Why sinks that cauldron? and what noise is this?
[Hautboys]

First Witch: Show!

Second Witch: Show!

Third Witch: Show!

All: Show his eyes, and grieve his heart;
Come like shadows, so depart!
[A show of Eight Kings, the last with a glass in his hand; Ghost of Banquo following]

Macbeth: Thou art too like the spirit of Banquo: down!
Thy crown does sear mine eye-balls. And thy hair,
Thou other gold-bound brow, is like the first.
A third is like the former. Filthy hags!
Why do you show me this? A fourth! Start, eyes!

What, will the line stretch out to the crack of doom?
Another yet! A seventh! I'll see no more:
And yet the eighth appears, who bears a glass
Which shows me many more; and some I see
That two-fold balls and treble scepters carry:
Horrible sight! Now, I see, 'tis true;
For the blood-bolter'd Banquo smiles upon me,
And points at them for his.
[Apparitions vanish]
What, is this so?
First Witch: Ay, sir, all this is so: but why
Stands Macbeth thus amazedly?
Come, sisters, cheer we up his sprites,
And show the best of our delights:
I'll charm the air to give a sound,
While you perform your antic round:
That this great king may kindly say,
Our duties did his welcome pay.
[Music. The witches dance and then vanish, with Hecate]
Macbeth: Where are they? Gone? Let this pernicious hour

Stand aye accursed in the calendar!

Come in, without there!

[Enter Lennox]

Lennox: What's your grace's will?

Macbeth: Saw you the weird sisters?

Lennox: No, my lord.

Macbeth: Came they not by you?

Lennox: No, indeed, my lord.

Macbeth: Infected be the air whereon they ride;
And damn'd all those that trust them! I did hear
The galloping of horse: who was't came by?

Lennox: 'Tis two or three, my lord, that bring you word
Macduff is fled to England.

Macbeth: Fled to England!

Lennox: Ay, my good lord.

Macbeth: Time, thou anticipatest my dread exploits:
The flighty purpose never is o'ertook
Unless the deed go with it; from this moment
The very firstlings of my heart shall be
The firstlings of my hand. And even now,
To crown my thoughts with acts, be it thought and

done:

The castle of Macduff I will surprise;

Seize upon Fife; give to the edge o' the sword

His wife, his babes, and all unfortunate souls

That trace him in his line. No boasting like a fool;

This deed I'll do before this purpose cool.

But no more sights!-Where are these gentlemen?

Come, bring me where they are.

[Exeunt]

Scene II. Fife. Macduff's castle.

[Enter Lady Macduff, her Son, and Ross]

Lady Macduff: What had he done, to make him fly the land?

Ross: You must have patience, madam.

Lady Macduff: He had none:

His flight was madness: when our actions do not,

Our fears do make us traitors.

Ross: You know not

Whether it was his wisdom or his fear.

Lady Macduff: Wisdom! to leave his wife, to leave his babes,

His mansion and his titles in a place
From whence himself does fly? He loves us not;
He wants the natural touch: for the poor wren,
The most diminutive of birds, will fight,
Her young ones in her nest, against the owl.
All is the fear and nothing is the love;
As little is the wisdom, where the flight
So runs against all reason.
Ross: My dearest coz,
I pray you, school yourself: but for your husband,
He is noble, wise, judicious, and best knows
The fits o' the season. I dare not speak
much further;
But cruel are the times, when we are traitors
And do not know ourselves, when we hold rumour
From what we fear, yet know not what we fear,
But float upon a wild and violent sea
Each way and move. I take my leave of you:
Shall not be long but I'll be here again:
Things at the worst will cease, or else climb
upward
To what they were before. My pretty cousin,
Blessing upon you!

Lady Macduff: Father'd he is, and yet he's fatherless.

Ross: I am so much a fool, should I stay longer,
It would be my disgrace and your discomfort:
I take my leave at once.

[Exit]

Lady Macduff: Sirrah, your father's dead;
And what will you do now? How will you live?

Son: As birds do, mother.

Lady Macduff: What, with worms and flies?

Son: With what I get, I mean; and so do they.

Lady Macduff: Poor bird! thou'ldst never fear the net nor lime,
The pitfall nor the gin.

Son: Why should I, mother? Poor birds they are not set for.
My father is not dead, for all your saying.

Lady Macduff: Yes, he is dead; how wilt thou do for a father?

Son: Nay, how will you do for a husband?

Lady Macduff: Why, I can buy me twenty at any market.

Son: Then you'll buy 'em to sell again.

Lady Macduff: Thou speak'st with all thy wit: and yet, i' faith,
With wit enough for thee.

Son: Was my father a traitor, mother?

Lady Macduff: Ay, that he was.

Son: What is a traitor?

Lady Macduff: Why, one that swears and lies.

Son: And be all traitors that do so?

Lady Macduff: Every one that does so is a traitor, and must be hanged.

Son: And must they all be hanged that swear and lie?

Lady Macduff: Every one.

Son: Who must hang them?

Lady Macduff: Why, the honest men.

Son: Then the liars and swearers are fools,
for there are liars and swearers enow to beat
the honest men and hang up them.

Lady Macduff: Now, God help thee, poor monkey!
But how wilt thou do for a father?

Son: If he were dead, you'd weep for
him: if you would not, it were a good sign
that I should quickly have a new father.

Lady Macduff: Poor prattler, how thou talk'st!

[Enter a Messenger]

Messenger: Bless you, fair dame! I am not to you known,
Though in your state of honour I am perfect.
I doubt some danger does approach you nearly:
If you will take a homely man's advice,
Be not found here; hence, with your little ones.
To fright you thus, methinks, I am too savage;
To do worse to you were fell cruelty,
Which is too nigh your person. Heaven preserve you!
I dare abide no longer.

[Exit]

Lady Macduff: Whither should I fly?
I have done no harm. But I remember now
I am in this earthly world; where to do harm
Is often laudable, to do good sometime
Accounted dangerous folly: why then, alas,
Do I put up that womanly defence,
To say I have done no harm?

[Enter Murderers]

What are these faces?

First Murderer: Where is your husband?

Lady Macduff: I hope, in no place so unsanctified

Where such as thou mayst find him.

First Murderer: He's a traitor.

Son: Thou liest, thou shag-hair'd villain!

First Murderer: What, you egg!

[Stabbing him]

Young fry of treachery!

Son: He has kill'd me, mother:

Run away, I pray you!

[Dies]

[Exit Lady Macduff, crying 'Murder!' Exeunt Murderers, following her]

Scene III. England. Before the King's Palace.

[Enter Malcolm and Macduff]

Malcolm: Let us seek out some desolate shade, and there

Weep our sad bosoms empty.

Macduff: Let us rather

Hold fast the mortal sword, and like good men

Bestride our down-fall'n birthdom: each new morn

New widows howl, new orphans cry, new sorrows
Strike heaven on the face, that it resounds
As if it felt with Scotland and yell'd out
Like syllable of dolour.
Malcolm: What I believe I'll wail,
What know believe, and what I can redress,
As I shall find the time to friend, I will.
What you have spoke, it may be so perchance.
This tyrant, whose sole name blisters our tongues,
Was once thought honest: you have loved him well.
He hath not touch'd you yet. I am young; but something
You may deserve of him through me, and wisdom
To offer up a weak poor innocent lamb
To appease an angry god.
Macduff: I am not treacherous.
Malcolm: But Macbeth is.
A good and virtuous nature may recoil
In an imperial charge. But I shall crave your pardon;
That which you are my thoughts cannot transpose:
Angels are bright still, though the brightest fell;

Though all things foul would wear the brows of grace,
Yet grace must still look so.

Macduff: I have lost my hopes.

Malcolm: Perchance even there where I did find my doubts.
Why in that rawness left you wife and child,
Those precious motives, those strong knots of love,
Without leave-taking? I pray you,
Let not my jealousies be your dishonours,
But mine own safeties. You may be rightly just,
Whatever I shall think.

Macduff: Bleed, bleed, poor country!
Great tyranny! lay thou thy basis sure,
For goodness dare not check thee: wear thou thy wrongs;
The title is affeer'd! Fare thee well, lord:
I would not be the villain that thou think'st
For the whole space that's in the tyrant's grasp,
And the rich East to boot.

Malcolm: Be not offended:
I speak not as in absolute fear of you.

I think our country sinks beneath the yoke;
It weeps, it bleeds; and each new day a gash
Is added to her wounds: I think withal
There would be hands uplifted in my right;
And here from gracious England have I offer
Of goodly thousands: but, for all this,
When I shall tread upon the tyrant's head,
Or wear it on my sword, yet my poor country
Shall have more vices than it had before,
More suffer and more sundry ways than ever,
By him that shall succeed.
Macduff: What should he be?
Malcolm: It is myself I mean: in whom I know
All the particulars of vice so grafted
That, when they shall be open'd, black Macbeth
Will seem as pure as snow, and the poor state
Esteem him as a lamb, being compared
With my confineless harms.
Macduff: Not in the legions
Of horrid hell can come a devil more damn'd
In evils to top Macbeth.
Malcolm: I grant him bloody,
Luxurious, avaricious, false, deceitful,

Sudden, malicious, smacking of every sin
That has a name: but there's no bottom, none,
In my voluptuousness: your wives, your daughters,
Your matrons and your maids, could not fill up
The cistern of my lust, and my desire
All continent impediments would o'erbear
That did oppose my will: better Macbeth
Than such an one to reign.
Macduff: Boundless intemperance
In nature is a tyranny; it hath been
The untimely emptying of the happy throne
And fall of many kings. But fear not yet
To take upon you what is yours: you may
Convey your pleasures in a spacious plenty,
And yet seem cold, the time you may so hoodwink.
We have willing dames enough: there cannot be
That vulture in you, to devour so many
As will to greatness dedicate themselves,
Finding it so inclined.
Malcolm: With this there grows
In my most ill-composed affection such
A stanchless avarice that, were I king,
I should cut off the nobles for their lands,

Desire his jewels and this other's house:
And my more-having would be as a sauce
To make me hunger more; that I should forge
Quarrels unjust against the good and loyal,
Destroying them for wealth.

Macduff: This avarice
Sticks deeper, grows with more pernicious root
Than summer-seeming lust, and it hath been
The sword of our slain kings: yet do not fear;
Scotland hath foisons to fill up your will.
Of your mere own: all these are portable,
With other graces weigh'd.

Malcolm: But I have none: the king-becoming graces,
As justice, verity, temperance, stableness,
Bounty, perseverance, mercy, lowliness,
Devotion, patience, courage, fortitude,
I have no relish of them, but abound
In the division of each several crime,
Acting it many ways. Nay, had I power, I should
Pour the sweet milk of concord into hell,
Uproar the universal peace, confound
All unity on earth.

Macduff: O Scotland, Scotland!

Malcolm: If such a one be fit to govern, speak:
I am as I have spoken.

Macduff: Fit to govern!
No, not to live. O nation miserable,
With an untitled tyrant bloody-scepter'd,
When shalt thou see thy wholesome days again,
Since that the truest issue of thy throne
By his own interdiction stands accursed,
And does blaspheme his breed? Thy royal father
Was a most sainted king: the queen that bore thee,
Oftener upon her knees than on her feet,
Died every day she lived. Fare thee well!
These evils thou repeat'st upon thyself
Have banish'd me from Scotland. O my breast,
Thy hope ends here!

Malcolm: Macduff, this noble passion,
Child of integrity, hath from my soul
Wiped the black scruples, reconciled my thoughts
To thy good truth and honour. Devilish Macbeth
By many of these trains hath sought to win me
Into his power, and modest wisdom plucks me

From over-credulous haste: but God above
Deal between thee and me! for even now
I put myself to thy direction, and
Unspeak mine own detraction, here abjure
The taints and blames I laid upon myself,
For strangers to my nature. I am yet
Unknown to woman, never was forsworn,
Scarcely have coveted what was mine own,
At no time broke my faith, would not betray
The devil to his fellow and delight
No less in truth than life: my first false speaking
Was this upon myself: what I am truly,
Is thine and my poor country's to command:
Whither indeed, before thy here-approach,
Old Siward, with ten thousand war-like men,
Already at a point, was setting forth.
Now we'll together; and the chance of goodness
Be like our warranted quarrel! Why are you silent?

Macduff: Such welcome and unwelcome things at once
'Tis hard to reconcile.

[Enter a Doctor]

Malcolm: Well; more anon. Comes the king forth, I

pray you?

Doctor: Ay, sir; there are a crew of wretched souls

That stay his cure: their malady convinces

The great assay of art; but at his touch,

Such sanctity hath heaven given his hand,

They presently amend.

Malcolm: I thank you, doctor.

[Exit Doctor]

Macduff: What's the disease he means?

Malcolm: 'Tis call'd the evil:

A most miraculous work in this good king;

Which often, since my here-remain in England,

I have seen him do. How he solicits heaven,

Himself best knows: but strangely-visited people,

All swoln and ulcerous, pitiful to the eye,

The mere despair of surgery, he cures,

Hanging a golden stamp about their necks,

Put on with holy prayers: and 'tis spoken,

To the succeeding royalty he leaves

The healing benediction. With this strange virtue,

He hath a heavenly gift of prophecy,

And sundry blessings hang about his throne,

That speak him full of grace.

Macduff: See, who comes here?

Malcolm: My countryman; but yet I know him not.

[Enter Ross]

Macduff: My ever-gentle cousin, welcome hither.

Malcolm: I know him now. Good God, betimes remove
The means that makes us strangers!

Ross: Sir, amen.

Macduff: Stands Scotland where it did?

Ross: Alas, poor country!
Almost afraid to know itself. It cannot
Be call'd our mother, but our grave; where nothing,
But who knows nothing, is once seen to smile;
Where sighs and groans and shrieks that rend the air
Are made, not mark'd; where violent sorrow seems
A modern ecstasy; the dead man's knell
Is there scarce ask'd for who; and good men's lives
Expire before the flowers in their caps,
Dying or ere they sicken.

Macduff: O, relation
Too nice, and yet too true!

Malcolm: What's the newest grief?

Ross: That of an hour's age doth hiss the speaker:
Each minute teems a new one.

Macduff: How does my wife?

Ross: Why, well.

Macduff: And all my children?

Ross: Well too.

Macduff: The tyrant has not batter'd at their peace?

Ross: No; they were well at peace when I did leave 'em.

Macduff: But not a niggard of your speech: how goes't?

Ross: When I came hither to transport the tidings,
Which I have heavily borne, there ran a rumour
Of many worthy fellows that were out;
Which was to my belief witness'd the rather,
For that I saw the tyrant's power a-foot:
Now is the time of help; your eye in Scotland
Would create soldiers, make our women fight,
To doff their dire distresses.

Malcolm: Be't their comfort

We are coming thither: gracious England hath
Lent us good Siward and ten thousand men;
An older and a better soldier none
That Christendom gives out.

Ross: Would I could answer
This comfort with the like! But I have words
That would be howl'd out in the desert air,
Where hearing should not latch them.

Macduff: What concern they?
The general cause? or is it a fee-grief
Due to some single breast?

Ross: No mind that's honest
But in it shares some woe; though the main part
Pertains to you alone.

Macduff: If it be mine,
Keep it not from me, quickly let me have it.

Ross: Let not your ears despise my tongue for ever,
Which shall possess them with the heaviest sound
That ever yet they heard.

Macduff: Hum! I guess at it.

Ross: Your castle is surprised; your wife and babes

Savagely slaughter'd: to relate the manner,

Were, on the quarry of these murder'd deer,

To add the death of you.

Malcolm: Merciful heaven!

What, man! ne'er pull your hat upon your brows;

Give sorrow words: the grief that does not speak

Whispers the o'er-fraught heart and bids it break.

Macduff: My children too?

Ross: Wife, children, servants, all

That could be found.

Macduff: And I must be from thence!

My wife kill'd too?

Ross: I have said.

Malcolm: Be comforted:

Let's make us medicines of our great revenge,

To cure this deadly grief.

Macduff: He has no children. All my pretty ones?

Did you say all? O hell-kite! All?

What, all my pretty chickens and their dam

At one fell swoop?

Malcolm: Dispute it like a man.

Macduff: I shall do so;

But I must also feel it as a man:

I cannot but remember such things were,
That were most precious to me. Did heaven look on,
And would not take their part? Sinful Macduff,
They were all struck for thee! Naught that I am,
Not for their own demerits, but for mine,
Fell slaughter on their souls. Heaven rest them now!

Malcolm: Be this the whetstone of your sword: let grief
Convert to anger; blunt not the heart, enrage it.

Macduff: O, I could play the woman with mine eyes
And braggart with my tongue! But, gentle heavens,
Cut short all intermission; front to front
Bring thou this fiend of Scotland and myself;
Within my sword's length set him; if he 'scape,
Heaven forgive him too!

Malcolm: This tune goes manly.
Come, go we to the king; our power is ready;
Our lack is nothing but our leave; Macbeth
Is ripe for shaking, and the powers above
Put on their instruments. Receive what cheer you

may:

The night is long that never finds the day.

[Exeunt]

Act IV: Notes

Act V

Scene I. Dunsinane. A Room in the Castle.

[Enter a Doctor of Physic and a Waiting-Gentlewoman]

Doctor: I have two nights watched with you, but can perceive no truth in your report. When was it she last walked?

Gentlewoman: Since his majesty went into the field, I have seen her rise from her bed, throw her night-gown upon her, unlock her closet, take forth paper, fold it, write upon't, read it, afterwards seal it, and again return to bed; yet all this while in a most fast sleep.

Doctor: A great perturbation in nature, to receive at once the benefit of sleep, and do the effects of watching! In this slumbery agitation, besides her walking and other actual performances, what, at any time, have you heard her say?

Gentlewoman: That, sir, which I will not report after her.

Doctor: You may to me: and 'tis most meet you

should.

Gentlewoman: Neither to you nor any one; having no witness to confirm my speech.

[Enter Lady Macbeth, with a taper]

Lo you, here she comes! This is her very guise; and, upon my life, fast asleep. Observe her; stand close.

Doctor: How came she by that light?

Gentlewoman: Why, it stood by her: she has light by her continually; 'tis her command.

Doctor: You see, her eyes are open.

Gentlewoman: Ay, but their sense is shut.

Doctor: What is it she does now? Look, how she rubs her hands.

Gentlewoman: It is an accustomed action with her, to seem thus washing her hands: I have known her continue in this a quarter of an hour.

Lady Macbeth: Yet here's a spot.

Doctor: Hark! she speaks: I will set down what comes from her, to satisfy my remembrance the more strongly.

Lady Macbeth: Out, damned spot! out, I say! One: two: why, then, 'tis time to do't. Hell is

murky! Fie, my lord, fie! a soldier, and afeard? What need we fear who knows it, when none can call our power to account? Yet who would have thought the old man to have had so much blood in him.

Doctor: Do you mark that?

Lady Macbeth: The thane of Fife had a wife: where is she now?

What, will these hands ne'er be clean? No more o' that, my lord, no more o' that: you mar all with this starting.

Doctor: Go to, go to; you have known what you should not.

Gentlewoman: She has spoke what she should not, I am sure of that: heaven knows what she has known.

Lady Macbeth: Here's the smell of the blood still: all the perfumes of Arabia will not sweeten this little hand. Oh, oh, oh!

Doctor: What a sigh is there! The heart is sorely charged.

Gentlewoman: I would not have such a heart in my bosom for the dignity of the whole body.

Doctor: Well, well, well.

Gentlewoman: Pray God it be, sir.

Doctor: This disease is beyond my practise: yet I have known those which have walked in their sleep who have died holily in their beds.

Lady Macbeth: Wash your hands, put on your nightgown; look not so pale. I tell you yet again, Banquo's buried; he cannot come out on's grave.

Doctor: Even so?

Lady Macbeth: To bed, to bed! there's knocking at the gate come, come, come, come, give me your hand. What's done cannot be undone. To bed, to bed, to bed!

[Exit]

Doctor: Will she go now to bed?

Gentlewoman: Directly.

Doctor: Foul whisperings are abroad: unnatural deeds
Do breed unnatural troubles: infected minds
To their deaf pillows will discharge their secrets:
More needs she the divine than the physician.
God, God forgive us all! Look after her;
Remove from her the means of all annoyance,

And still keep eyes upon her. So, good night:
My mind she has mated, and amazed my sight.
I think, but dare not speak.

Gentlewoman: Good night, good doctor.

[Exeunt]

Scene II. The Country near Dunsinane.

[Drum and colours. Enter Menteith, Caithness, Angus, Lennox, and Soldiers]

Menteith: The English power is near, led on by Malcolm,
His uncle Siward and the good Macduff:
Revenges burn in them; for their dear causes
Would to the bleeding and the grim alarm
Excite the mortified man.

Angus: Near Birnam wood
Shall we well meet them; that way are they coming.

Caithness: Who knows if Donalbain be with his brother?

Lennox: For certain, sir, he is not: I have a file
Of all the gentry: there is Siward's son,

And many unrough youths that even now
Protest their first of manhood.
Menteith: What does the tyrant?
Caithness: Great Dunsinane he strongly fortifies:
Some say he's mad; others that lesser hate him
Do call it valiant fury: but, for certain,
He cannot buckle his distemper'd cause
Within the belt of rule.
Angus: Now does he feel
His secret murders sticking on his hands;
Now minutely revolts upbraid his faith-breach;
Those he commands move only in command,
Nothing in love: now does he feel his title
Hang loose about him, like a giant's robe
Upon a dwarfish thief.
Menteith: Who then shall blame
His pester'd senses to recoil and start,
When all that is within him does condemn
Itself for being there?
Caithness: Well, march we on,
To give obedience where 'tis truly owed:
Meet we the medicine of the sickly weal,
And with him pour we in our country's purge

Each drop of us.

Lennox: Or so much as it needs,
To dew the sovereign flower and drown the weeds.
Make we our march towards Birnam. [Exeunt, marching]

Scene III. Dunsinane. A Room in the Castle.

[Enter Macbeth, Doctor, and Attendants]

Macbeth: Bring me no more reports; let them fly all:
Till Birnam wood remove to Dunsinane,
I cannot taint with fear. What's the boy Malcolm?
Was he not born of woman? The spirits that know
All mortal consequences have pronounced me thus:
'Fear not, Macbeth; no man that's born of woman
Shall e'er have power upon thee.' Then fly, false thanes,
And mingle with the English epicures:
The mind I sway by and the heart I bear
Shall never sag with doubt nor shake with fear.

[Enter a Servant]

The devil damn thee black, thou cream-faced loon!

Where got'st thou that goose look?

Servant: There is ten thousand -

Macbeth: Geese, villain?

Servant: Soldiers, sir.

Macbeth: Go prick thy face, and over-red thy fear,

Thou lily-liver'd boy. What soldiers, patch?

Death of thy soul! those linen cheeks of thine

Are counsellors to fear. What soldiers, whey-face?

Servant: The English force, so please you.

Macbeth: Take thy face hence.

[Exit Servant]

Seyton! I am sick at heart,

When I behold - Seyton, I say! - This push

Will cheer me ever, or disseat me now.

I have lived long enough: my way of life

Is fall'n into the sear, the yellow leaf;

And that which should accompany old age,

As honour, love, obedience, troops of friends,

I must not look to have; but, in their stead,

Curses, not loud but deep, mouth-honour, breath,

Which the poor heart would fain deny, and dare

not. Seyton!

[Enter Seyton]

Seyton: What is your gracious pleasure?

Macbeth: What news more?

Seyton: All is confirm'd, my lord, which was reported.

Macbeth: I'll fight till from my bones my flesh be hack'd.

Give me my armour.

Seyton: 'Tis not needed yet.

Macbeth: I'll put it on.

Send out more horses; skirr the country round;

Hang those that talk of fear. Give me mine armour.

How does your patient, doctor?

Doctor: Not so sick, my lord,

As she is troubled with thick-coming fancies,

That keep her from her rest.

Macbeth: Cure her of that.

Canst thou not minister to a mind diseased,

Pluck from the memory a rooted sorrow,

Raze out the written troubles of the brain

And with some sweet oblivious antidote

Cleanse the stuff'd bosom of that perilous stuff

Which weighs upon the heart?

Doctor: Therein the patient
Must minister to himself.

Macbeth: Throw physic to the dogs; I'll none of it.
Come, put mine armour on; give me my staff.
Seyton, send out. Doctor, the thanes fly from me.
Come, sir, dispatch. If thou couldst, doctor, cast
The water of my land, find her disease,
And purge it to a sound and pristine health,
I would applaud thee to the very echo,
That should applaud again.-Pull't off, I say.-
What rhubarb, senna, or what purgative drug,
Would scour these English hence? Hear'st thou of them?

Doctor: Ay, my good lord; your royal preparation
Makes us hear something.

Macbeth: Bring it after me.
I will not be afraid of death and bane,
Till Birnam forest come to Dunsinane.

Doctor: [Aside] Were I from Dunsinane away and clear,
Profit again should hardly draw me here.

[Exeunt]

Scene IV. Country near Birnam Wood.

[Enter with Drum and colours Malcolm, Siward and Young Siward, Macduff, Menteith, Caithness, Angus, Lennox, Ross, and Soldiers, marching]

Malcolm: Cousins, I hope the days are near at hand
That chambers will be safe.

Menteith: We doubt it nothing.

Siward: What wood is this before us?

Menteith: The wood of Birnam.

Malcolm: Let every soldier hew him down a bough
And bear't before him: thereby shall we shadow
The numbers of our host and make discovery
Err in report of us.

Soldiers: It shall be done.

Siward: We learn no other but the confident tyrant
Keeps still in Dunsinane, and will endure
Our setting down before 't.

Malcolm: 'Tis his main hope:
For where there is advantage to be given,
Both more and less have given him the revolt,
And none serve with him but constrained things

Whose hearts are absent too.

Macduff: Let our just censures

Attend the true event, and put we on

Industrious soldiership.

Siward: The time approaches

That will with due decision make us know

What we shall say we have and what we owe.

Thoughts speculative their unsure hopes relate,

But certain issue strokes must arbitrate:

Towards which advance the war. [Exeunt, marching]

Scene V. Dunsinane. Within the Castle.

[Enter with Drum and colours Macbeth, Seyton, and Soldiers]

Macbeth: Hang out our banners on the outward walls;

The cry is still 'They come:' our castle's strength

Will laugh a siege to scorn: here let them lie

Till famine and the ague eat them up:

Were they not forced with those that should be ours,

We might have met them dareful, beard to beard,
And beat them backward home.
A cry of women within
What is that noise?
Seyton: It is the cry of women, my good lord.
[Exit]
Macbeth: I have almost forgot the taste of fears;
The time has been, my senses would have cool'd
To hear a night-shriek; and my fell of hair
Would at a dismal treatise rouse and stir
As life were in't: I have supp'd full with horrors;
Direness, familiar to my slaughterous thoughts
Cannot once start me.
[Re-enter Seyton]
Wherefore was that cry?
Seyton: The queen, my lord, is dead.
Macbeth: She should have died hereafter;
There would have been a time for such a word.
To-morrow, and to-morrow, and to-morrow,
Creeps in this petty pace from day to day
To the last syllable of recorded time,
And all our yesterdays have lighted fools
The way to dusty death. Out, out, brief candle!

Life's but a walking shadow, a poor player
That struts and frets his hour upon the stage
And then is heard no more: it is a tale
Told by an idiot, full of sound and fury,
Signifying nothing.
[Enter a Messenger]
Thou comest to use thy tongue; thy story quickly.
Messenger: Gracious my lord,
I should report that which I say I saw,
But know not how to do it.
Macbeth: Well, say, sir.
Messenger: As I did stand my watch upon the hill,
I look'd toward Birnam, and anon, methought,
The wood began to move.
Macbeth: Liar and slave!
Messenger: Let me endure your wrath, if't be not so:
Within this three mile may you see it coming;
I say, a moving grove.
Macbeth: If thou speak'st false,
Upon the next tree shalt thou hang alive,
Till famine cling thee: if thy speech be sooth,
I care not if thou dost for me as much.

I pull in resolution, and begin
To doubt the equivocation of the fiend
That lies like truth: 'Fear not, till Birnam wood
Do come to Dunsinane': and now a wood
Comes toward Dunsinane. Arm, arm, and out!
If this which he avouches does appear,
There is nor flying hence nor tarrying here.
I 'gin to be aweary of the sun,
And wish the estate o' the world were now
undone.
Ring the alarum-bell! Blow, wind! come, wrack!
At least we'll die with harness on our back.
[Exeunt]

Scene VI. The Same. A Plain before the Castle.

[Enter with Drum and colours Malcolm, Siward,
Macduff, etc and their Army, with boughs]
Malcolm: Now near enough: your leafy screens
throw down.
And show like those you are. You, worthy uncle,
Shall, with my cousin, your right-noble son,
Lead our first battle: worthy Macduff and we

Shall take upon 's what else remains to do,
According to our order.
Siward: Fare you well.
Do we but find the tyrant's power to-night,
Let us be beaten, if we cannot fight.
Macduff: Make all our trumpets speak; give them all breath,
Those clamorous harbingers of blood and death.
[Exeunt]

SCENE VII. The Same. Another Part of the Plain.

[Alarums. Enter Macbeth]
Macbeth: They have tied me to a stake; I cannot fly,
But, bear-like, I must fight the course. What's he
That was not born of woman? Such a one
Am I to fear, or none.
[Enter Young Siward]
Young Siward: What is thy name?
Macbeth: Thou'lt be afraid to hear it.
Young Siward: No; though thou call'st thyself a

hotter name

Than any is in hell.

Macbeth: My name's Macbeth.

Young Siward: The devil himself could not pronounce a title

More hateful to mine ear.

Macbeth: No, nor more fearful.

Young Siward: Thou liest, abhorred tyrant; with my sword

I'll prove the lie thou speak'st.

[They fight and Young Siward is slain]

Macbeth: Thou wast born of woman

But swords I smile at, weapons laugh to scorn,

Brandish'd by man that's of a woman born.

[Exit]

[Alarums. Enter Macduff]

Macduff: That way the noise is. Tyrant, show thy face!

If thou be'st slain and with no stroke of mine,

My wife and children's ghosts will haunt me still.

I cannot strike at wretched kerns, whose arms

Are hired to bear their staves: either thou, Macbeth,

Or else my sword with an unbatter'd edge
I sheathe again undeeded. There thou shouldst be;
By this great clatter, one of greatest note
Seems bruited. Let me find him, fortune!
And more I beg not.
[Exit. Alarums]
[Enter Malcolm and Old Siward]
Siward: This way, my lord; the castle's gently render'd:
The tyrant's people on both sides do fight;
The noble thanes do bravely in the war;
The day almost itself professes yours,
And little is to do.
Malcolm: We have met with foes
That strike beside us.
Siward: Enter, sir, the castle.
[Exeunt. Alarums]

Scene VIII. Another Part of the Plain.

[Enter Macbeth]
Macbeth: Why should I play the Roman fool, and

die

On mine own sword? whiles I see lives, the

gashes

Do better upon them.

[Enter Macduff]

Macduff: Turn, hell-hound, turn!

Macbeth: Of all men else I have avoided thee:

But get thee back; my soul is too much charged

With blood of thine already.

Macduff: I have no words:

My voice is in my sword: thou bloodier villain

Than terms can give thee out!

[They fight]

Macbeth: Thou losest labour:

As easy mayst thou the intrenchant air

With thy keen sword impress as make me bleed:

Let fall thy blade on vulnerable crests;

I bear a charmed life, which must not yield,

To one of woman born.

Macduff: Despair thy charm;

And let the angel whom thou still hast served

Tell thee, Macduff was from his mother's womb

Untimely ripp'd.

Macbeth: Accursed be that tongue that tells me so,

For it hath cow'd my better part of man!

And be these juggling fiends no more believed,

That palter with us in a double sense;

That keep the word of promise to our ear,

And break it to our hope. I'll not fight with thee.

Macduff: Then yield thee, coward,

And live to be the show and gaze o' the time:

We'll have thee, as our rarer monsters are,

Painted on a pole, and underwrit,

'Here may you see the tyrant.'

Macbeth: I will not yield,

To kiss the ground before young Malcolm's feet,

And to be baited with the rabble's curse.

Though Birnam wood be come to Dunsinane,

And thou opposed, being of no woman born,

Yet I will try the last. Before my body

I throw my warlike shield. Lay on, Macduff,

And damn'd be him that first cries, 'Hold, enough!'

[Exeunt, fighting. Alarums]

[Retreat. Flourish. Re-enter, with drum and colours, Malcolm, Old Siward, Ross, Thanes, and

Soldiers]

Malcolm: I would the friends we miss were safe arrived.

Siward: Some must go off: and yet, by these I see,

So great a day as this is cheaply bought.

Malcolm: Macduff is missing, and your noble son.

Ross: Your son, my lord, has paid a soldier's debt:

He only lived but till he was a man;

The which no sooner had his prowess confirm'd

In the unshrinking station where he fought,

But like a man he died.

Siward: Then he is dead?

Ross: Ay, and brought off the field: your cause of sorrow

Must not be measured by his worth, for then

It hath no end.

Siward: Had he his hurts before?

Ross: Ay, on the front.

Siward: Why then, God's soldier be he!

Had I as many sons as I have hairs,

I would not wish them to a fairer death:

And so, his knell is knoll'd.

Malcolm: He's worth more sorrow,
And that I'll spend for him.
Siward: He's worth no more
They say he parted well, and paid his score:
And so, God be with him! Here comes newer comfort.
[Re-enter Macduff, with Macbeth's head]
Macduff: Hail, king! for so thou art: behold, where stands
The usurper's cursed head: the time is free:
I see thee compass'd with thy kingdom's pearl,
That speak my salutation in their minds;
Whose voices I desire aloud with mine:
Hail, King of Scotland!
All: Hail, King of Scotland!
[Flourish]
Malcolm: We shall not spend a large expense of time
Before we reckon with your several loves,
And make us even with you. My thanes and kinsmen,
Henceforth be earls, the first that ever Scotland
In such an honour named. What's more to do,

Which would be planted newly with the time,
As calling home our exiled friends abroad
That fled the snares of watchful tyranny;
Producing forth the cruel ministers
Of this dead butcher and his fiend-like queen,
Who, as 'tis thought, by self and violent hands
Took off her life; this, and what needful else
That calls upon us, by the grace of Grace,
We will perform in measure, time and place:
So, thanks to all at once and to each one,
Whom we invite to see us crown'd at Scone.
[Flourish. Exeunt]

Act V: Notes

Glossary of Literary Terms

Alliteration: The occurrence of identical sounds, most often at the beginning of words e.g. "From forth the fatal loins of these two foes"

Allusion: An indirect reference to something

Anaphora: Repetition of the same word or phrase at the beginning of consecutive lines

Antagonist: The **protagonist**'s main adversary.

Antithesis: A person or thing that is the opposite of something else

Aside: A character's remark that is only meant to be heard by the audience but unheard by other characters in the play

Assonance: The resemblance of sounds between vowels of words in close proximity to one another

Blank verse: **Poetry** written with a regular **metre** but unrhymed, almost always in **iambic pentameter**

Climax: The dramatic end to the main **plot**. This is usually followed by **falling action**

Couplet: Two successive rhyming lines

Dramatic monologue: A poem in the form of a speech of an individual character

Euphemism: A gentle way of expressing something unpleasant

Falling Action: The section of a story following the **climax** but before the very end of the story

Foil: A character providing a contrast with another

Foot: A combination of stressed and unstressed syllables

Heroic couplet: a pair of rhyming **iambic pentameters**

Hyperbole: Exaggerated statements not meant to be taken literally

Iambic pentameter: A line of verse with five metrical feet, each consisting of one unstressed syllable followed by one stressed syllable

Imagery: A visually descriptive use of language

Internal rhyme: A rhyme involving a word in the middle of a line

Metaphor: A figure of speech that applies words to describe something in a non-literal way (e.g. *coal black eyes*). Metaphors do not use the words "like" or "as". If these words are used it is a **simile** (e.g. *eyes as black as coal*, or *eyes like black coal*).

Metre: The basic rhythmic structure of a verse or lines in a verse

Motif: An image or idea that runs through a play or novel

Onomatopoeia: A word that resembles the sound it is describing e.g. cuckoo, woof, burp, etc

Oxymoron: A figure of speech containing contradictory words, e.g. deafening silence

Paradox: A statement that contradicts itself e.g "This sentence is not true"

Personification: Attributing human characteristics to inanimate things

Plot: The events that make up the main part of a story

Poetry: Rhymed or rhythmic text

Pronoun: Referring to a person or thing, e.g. I, you, she, this, that

Prose: Written or spoken language without rhyme or rhythm

Protagonist: The lead character

Quatrain: A **stanza** of four lines

Refrain: A word or series of words repeated at intervals within a poem

Shakespearean sonnet: A fourteen-line poem written in **iambic pentameter**, composed of three **quatrains** of four lines each and a **couplet** rhyming: abab cdcd efef gg.

Simile: A figure of speech containing “as” or “like” to describe something in a non-literal way (e.g. eyes like black coal). If the words “like” or “as” are not used then it is a **metaphor** (e.g. coal black eyes).

Soliloquy: A speech spoken by a character when alone, revealing their innermost thoughts

Sonnet: A fourteen-line poem. See also **Shakespearean sonnet**

Stanza: A group of poetic lines resembling paragraphs in **prose**

Sub-plot: A plot separate to the main **plot**

Syntax: The arrangement of words and phrases within a sentence

Tragic Hero: Generally the **protagonist** whose flaws or mistakes lead to their downfall

Macbeth Glossary

Acheron – Hell
Ague – Disease
Aroint – Go away
Augur – To foresee or predict the future
Avouch – Justify
Bark – A small ship
Beldams – Witches
Bellona – Goddess of war
Benison – Blessing
Bodements – Omens
Compunction – Feeling of guilt after committing a crime
Corporal – Bodily or physical
Coz – Cousin
Dudgeon – Ill humour
Enow – Enough
Equivocation – To lie or deceive
Fenny – Living in the marshes
Foison – Rich harvest
Germens – Seeds
Golgotha – Site of Jesus's crucifixion
Gorgon – Mythical monster that turns its beholders to stone
Graymalkin – Grey cat
Harbinger – Forerunner
Hecate – Goddess of witchcraft
Holp – Helped
Hyrcan – Someone from Hyrcania, now part of Iran
Incarnadine – Crimson
Lees – Dregs

Maw – Appetite
Metaphysical – Supernatural
Mettle – Courage
Minion – Servant
Parricide – The killing of a parent
Rancour – Bitterness
Regicide – The killing of a monarch
Runyon – Old woman or hag
Sooth – Truthfully
Surcease – Death
Surfeited – Drunk
Trains – Trick
Verities – True predictions
Vizards – Masks
Warder – A guard or jailer
Wassail – Mulled wine
Yesty – Frothing